CHRISTINA GARBUTT

◆

MYSTERY AT MORWENNA BAY

Complete and Unabridged

LINFORD
Leicester

First published in Great Britain in 2018

First Linford Edition
published 2019

A catalogue record for this book is available
from the British Library.

ISBN 978–1–4448–4289–0

Published by
F. A. Thorpe (Publishing)
Anstey, Leicestershire

Set by Words & Graphics Ltd.
Anstey, Leicestershire
Printed and bound in Great Britain by
T. J. International Ltd., Padstow, Cornwall

This book is printed on acid-free paper

WITHDRAWN

MYSTERY AT
MORWENNA BAY

Budding criminologist Ellie is glad to help her gran recuperate after an accident, expecting to spend a quiet month in rural Wales before heading back to London to submit her PhD. But she's bemused to find that she's something of a celebrity in the village, and expected to help solve a series of devastating livestock thefts for which there is no shortage of suspects. She's also wrong-footed by the friendly overtures of handsome young farmer Tom — even though a relationship is absolutely the last thing she wants or needs . . .

1

Ellie tugged the edges of her cardigan and hugged the material closer to her body. The early summer sun was giving way to a chilly evening and the shady car park was cooling rapidly.

She glanced at her watch. Her coach had been slightly early but even so, her lift was now five minutes late. Had she been forgotten?

A breeze stirred her long, dark ponytail and she shuddered. The cardigan wasn't up to keeping her warm. Carefully she unzipped the top of her suitcase and wiggled her fingers inside, searching for her jacket. Her fingers caught on the hood and she tugged on it. After a few moments of wrestling she managed to pull it out of the small opening.

She slipped it on and then, using her suitcase as a makeshift seat, propped herself up. High-heeled boots had been a mistake on the long journey with its many changes and long waits but she hadn't wanted to leave her favourite shoes at home and they were too long to fit in her case.

She tilted her head and listened for the sound of an approaching car but the only sound she could pick out was a blackbird's evening song, sung high above her in a nearby tree.

It had been years since she'd stayed with Gran and Grandad in this corner of Wales. Her childhood memories of this place were full of endless sun and the heady freedom of exploration without supervision. She'd grown bored during her teenage years, and at fourteen had put her foot down and refused to come and stay any more.

Her heart tugged as she thought of Grandad, with his wonky walk and his massive bear hugs. She'd thought he'd live forever, but suddenly he was gone and she realised there was so much she'd never asked him. She pushed aside the guilt and grief and focused on the fact that she was here for Gran now. That was all that mattered.

She glanced at her watch again. Where was Tom? Her gran's neighbour should be here by now. She hadn't thought to ask for his mobile number to check he was still coming for her.

Would the man she'd been so fond of still hold the same fascination for her as he had when she was a child? His life on the farm was so different from her upbringing with her parents, whose work took them all over the world. He and his wife, Lynn, had been endlessly patient with her whenever she'd wandered around their farm talking to all the animals and generally getting in everyone's way. She was looking forward to seeing them both again — if, that is, Tom ever turned up.

A red Volvo estate encrusted with mud over the wheel arches, pulled into the car park and stopped directly in the space in front of her. She stood up hoping this was finally Tom. The driver's door snapped open and a young man leaped out.

'Hi, Ellie,' he said brightly. 'Wow, you look exactly the same as I remember. Is this your only case? You've not brought much. Let's get it in the car.'

He strode purposefully round to the boot, popped it open, slung in her suitcase and slammed it shut. He was putting one long leg into the footwell of the driver's side before he realised that Ellie hadn't moved.

'Are you getting in?' he asked.

'Um,' said Ellie cautiously, 'who are you?'

'Tom,' he said, as if it was blindingly obvious. 'Your Gran's neighbour.'

Ellie shook her head. 'Tom's got to be at least sixty and you're maybe twenty-four,' she said accusingly.

Tom grinned. 'I'm twenty-seven, same as you. The Tom you're thinking of is my dad — also called Tom — who took early retirement last year. I've taken the farm over. Don't you remember me?'

4

When Ellie didn't reply, he added, 'I'm crushed. I remember you very well.'

He didn't look crushed. With one hand resting on the roof of his car and the other on his hip, he looked very amused. Despite his charming smile Ellie was still wary about getting into a car with a stranger, especially one whose arms looked as though they could snap her in two without any trouble.

She had a vague recollection of Tom's son, a thin, sullen boy scowling around in the background during her last visit thirteen years ago but this didn't match up with this tall, broad-shouldered, grinning man in front of her. She had an inkling her parents had thought of him as a troublemaker.

'You're never Tearaway Tom,' she said finally.

He flung back his head and laughed.

'I haven't been called that in years,' he said, 'but yes, that's me. I promise I'm a reformed character. Come on,

5

let's get going. Your gran's promised to feed me in return for fetching you and I'm starving.'

He started to get back into the car but stopped and winked at her when she still didn't move.

'I promise I'll deliver you in one piece,' he said.

He folded the rest of his long body into the car and closed the door with a solid bang.

Ellie rummaged inside her handbag and felt the cold edges of her hairspray. Feeling reassured that she had something to use as a makeshift weapon she made her way around the car to the passenger door, which creaked on its hinges as she pulled it open.

The interior was surprisingly tidy and she sank gratefully into the soft leather. After five hours squashed into a lumpy coach seat, this was bliss. The car grumbled to life and Tom pulled out of the car park and into a narrow country lane.

Tom drove sedately through the

winding roads, a soft smile playing over his lips. His long fingers tapped the wheel in time to a song on the radio and Ellie tried to study him without looking at him directly.

In her memory Tom, whose existence she'd forgotten entirely until five minutes ago, was a dark shadow in semi-Goth clothing and with jet-black hair, hanging annoyingly into his eyes. This man had ash-blond hair cut short in no particular style, he was wearing a faded red checked shirt open at the collar and pale jeans. He couldn't be more different.

His smile turned into a wide grin.

'I can practically hear you thinking,' he said. 'Are you still unconvinced I'm Tom? My wallet's in the back if you want to check my identity.'

'I thought you had black hair,' she said.

'Ah, you must be remembering my angst phase. Everything was black, my hair, my clothes and even, to my parents' horror, my bedroom. It only lasted a year but my parents love to get out the photos whenever they feel the need to embarrass me.'

Ellie smiled and slightly relaxed her death grip on her handbag.

'Of course I could be lying. Perhaps I murdered Tom and stole his identity, although if I'd gone to the bother of killing someone, surely I'd have chosen a victim with a better car.'

'What's wrong with this car?' she asked, alarmed at the thought of being stranded in the middle of nowhere after a whole day of travelling.

'Nothing — but I'd prefer a Maserati, given the choice.'

They drove the next mile in silence.

'Your gran's so pleased you're coming to stay while she recuperates,' Tom said finally. 'She was showing me your itinerary this morning. It's pretty full up.'

Ellie's chest tightened. When Gran had fallen and broken her leg in two places, she hadn't hesitated to take some time off work. With Dad and

Mum working abroad, she was Gran's only relative in Britain and she wasn't about to leave her in the hands of some random carer.

It didn't mean that she was going to be able to take a break from work while she did it. Far from it. As well as lecturing in criminology, she'd spent the last four years working towards a PhD and now it was time to write up all her research.

Her supervisor was expecting at least two draft chapters by mid-September and so far, even though it was July, she'd written nothing. Every time she opened up a Word document she became panicky and had to shut her computer down again. Her PhD was all part of her career plan, so it really was time for her to get her head down and get it done. Whenever Gran didn't need her, she was going to be writing. Sadly that didn't leave much time for socialising.

'I'm prepared for all the cooking, lifting and . . . well, everything that's involved. It won't be a problem,' she said, more confidently than she felt. She hadn't cooked anything more compli-cated than a slice of toast in years — but how hard could it be?

'Um, what will you be lifting?' asked Tom.

'Gran of course,' she said.

'Why on earth would you be lifting her? What are you planning to do over the next few weeks?' Tom grinned.

'She's seventy-five and she's not able to use one of her legs. She's going to need lifting,' growled Ellie, getting annoyed with his near constant grin.

Tom slowed a little to take a sharp turn into a steep hill.

'Do you really think,' he said, once they were straight again, 'that a little thing like a broken leg is going to keep Laura Potts down? I didn't see anything about lifting on the list, but there was quite a lot about meeting up with the Lavender Ladies — and who knows what they get up to when there's no one around to see?'

Tom glanced across at her and winked.

Ellie frowned. Who were the Lavender Ladies and why would she be spending so much time with them?

'According to your Gran,' Tom continued, 'they're all really looking forward to having a real-life criminal investigator in their midst. I think there's some hope that you'll give a talk on solving crime in London.'

Ellie glared at him. His lips were pressed tightly together, suppressing the grin she could see dancing in his eyes. Did she want to give him the satisfaction of knowing he was winding her up by asking him what on earth he was talking about? Or did she want to arrive at Gran's unprepared?

'I'm a lecturer in criminology, not a police officer. I've never done any criminal investigating,' she said lightly.

She quite often met this confusion from people who didn't understand that you could study the theory behind crime but not be involved in law enforcement. She loved her job and couldn't imagine changing it to catching criminals; that sounded far too dangerous.

'Who are the Lavender Ladies?' she asked.

'They're a local group of women, who meet up twice a month at The Ship to socialise and have a bit of fun. Kind of like the WI, I suppose.

'Do you remember The Ship? No? I guess you'd have been too young to care about pubs when you stayed before. It's one of the two pubs in Morwenna Bay and by far and away the best. I'm sure you'll spend some time there while you're visiting. The Lavender Ladies go there unless they have a special guest like yourself, and then they go to the community hall first. You can hear the laughter from two streets away. Pretty certain you'll enjoy it.'

Ellie made no comment. It was unlikely she'd have time to meet up with these ladies no matter how much fun they were. She was here to help

Gran with washing, dressing and getting about. She was going to spend the time getting to know her grandmother again while frantically writing whenever she had the opportunity.

Tom's car finally turned into Gran's courtyard and came to a stop outside the long bungalow.

'You're wrong about Gran,' she said defensively. 'I expect she'll be back at this Lavender Ladies' group and whatever else she does when her leg's healed but we're going to have a quiet time while I'm here.'

'There's never a quiet moment in Morwenna Bay,' he said. Before she could reply, he added, 'I'll get your case.'

Ellie stretched as she got out of the car. It was so good to finally be here after all that travelling. Gran's thatched bungalow looked exactly the same as it did in her memories. A vibrant red clematis climbed around the wooden front door and the whitewashed walls shone in the last of the day's sunlight.

13

'Darling,' said Gran, appearing in her doorway, her shoulder-length, snow-white hair sparkling in the sun's rays. Her leg was cast from the hip down and she sat in a wheelchair with the leg sticking out at an awkward angle. A tall, thin woman whom Ellie recognised as Gran's good friend, Jude, stood behind her, holding on to the handles of the chair.

Ellie was suddenly running. How had she managed to stay away for so long? Her arms went around Gran and she buried her face in her neck, inhaling her soft, floral scent. She felt Gran's strong arms wrap around her middle as she returned the hug.

'Gran,' Ellie said, when she finally let go, 'how are you feeling?'

'Me?' asked Gran, sounding surprised. 'I'm very well, my love. But you must be exhausted after all that travelling. Come in and eat — you too, Tom. I expect you're both ravenous.'

They all shuffled slowly into Gran's hallway. The darkness inside was disorientating but the place still smelled the same as Ellie remembered, a delicious combination of home-cooked food and Gran's perfume.

'Where would you like Ellie's suitcase put?' Tom asked.

'Ellie's room is the last one on the left,' Gran said, gesturing to a corridor leading off from the main hallway.

'I can see to it,' said Ellie.

Gran and Tom ignored her and Tom headed off in the direction Gran had indicated.

'Now, let's get you settled with a cup of tea before dinner's ready, because we need to tell you all about our morning, don't we, Jude?'

'We do, Laura,' answered Jude as she pushed Gran into the lounge.

'Oh?' said Ellie, stopping to look at a picture of Grandad grinning proudly among canes of home-grown runner beans. She heard Tom's footsteps coming up behind her so she turned and followed Jude's retreating back.

'Yes, darling,' said Gran as Ellie

15

stepped into the lounge to join them. 'You see there's been a theft — and,' said Gran, proudly, 'I just know you're the one who can solve it.'

Ellie didn't need to see Tom's face to know that he was grinning.

2

Tom and Jude counted as formal guests, so they all sat around Gran's oak table to eat dinner. The table was almost as large as Ellie's entire kitchen and the four of them had clustered around one end so they didn't have to shout to make themselves heard.

Ellie watched in fascination as another forkful of chicken coated in a rich tomato sauce disappeared into Tom's mouth. He was eating Gran's chicken stew as if he might never see food again.

'This meal is heavenly, Mrs Potts,' said Tom.

'Tom, I've told you a million times to call me Laura,' said Gran, beaming at the compliment.

'People will think I've designs on you if I call you by your first name,' said Tom as he began to methodically scrape his plate clean, obviously not wanting to leave an atom of the meal uneaten.

Gran laughed. 'If only I were a few years younger . . . '

Ellie ignored their flirting and pushed her last mouthful of creamy mashed potato onto her fork. Tom was right, this meal was divine. After months of living on microwave meals and take-aways it felt so good to have fresh vegetables running through her system again. She took a bite of the mash and closed her eyes to savour the soft, silky texture.

'Any thoughts on the case, then, Ellie?' asked Tom.

Ellie opened her eyes and glared at him. His constant teasing was spoiling her appreciation of the good food. His blue eyes were sparkling with sup-pressed laughter. She didn't understand why he was getting so much enjoyment from the slightly awkward situation.

Ellie was an academic who taught students about crime scenes but didn't go to them herself. She looked at crime from a theoretical perspective and she was good at what she did. But for some reason it seemed that, in her prolonged absence, Gran had painted Ellie as some sort of super-sleuth, a female Sherlock Holmes, who could crack any case. Gran was so proud of Ellie's work that she couldn't bring herself to explain the reality and now Gran wanted her to solve something that, in all probability, was due to absentmind-edness rather than anything nefarious.

Earlier Jude had taken Gran to the nearby town to get a few last-minute things for Ellie's visit. Ellie wished they hadn't gone. The whole point of Ellie coming to stay was for her to be a help to Gran, not to make things more stressful. And this trip definitely had added stress. At some point during the afternoon Jude's handbag had disap-peared. Jude had only realised when she'd wanted to pay Gran back for some Penhaligon soap.

There was only a small amount of

cash in the bag, but it was a Burberry handbag and a present from her husband. Jude desperately wanted it back. They'd phoned around the shops they'd visited but to no avail. After telling Ellie their story, Gran had looked at Ellie with such hopeful pride that Ellie found herself saying she'd look into the problem after dinner.

'Any thoughts about what case, Tom?' she answered him.

'You had your eyes closed with such a thoughtful look on your face. I thought you might be solving the case of the missing handbag.'

'I was just enjoying the food. How did you manage to make all this, Gran?' Ellie asked, changing the subject as fast as she could.

She didn't want to let Gran down, but she also didn't relish the idea of traipsing around town looking for a Burberry handbag and the inevitable disappointment when she returned empty-handed. If Jude had left such an expensive bag hanging around, it was probably long gone.

'Oh, this is nothing,' said Gran. 'I'd made up a few batches of stew before my accident. I always have a few meals frozen. They come in handy when I have the girls over for dinner. I've done the same with today's pudding.'

'Would that be the apple pie I saw in the kitchen earlier?' asked Tom.

'Yes, it is,' said Gran. 'We'll have some custard with it too.'

'Excellent, apple pie's my favourite,' said Tom. 'I'll clear up the dishes and bring it through.'

He stacked up the empty plates and carried them through to the kitchen. Gran and Jude leaned forward to watch him go. Gran caught Ellie's eye and her cheeks turned a rosy pink.

'You're never too old to appreciate a fine set of shoulders,' Gran whispered defiantly.

Ellie laughed.

'They'd make a beautiful couple,' said Jude to Gran.

Ellie stopped laughing. Was Jude

talking about her and Tom? The last thing she needed was Gran getting romantic ideas in her head. There was no way Ellie would become a farmer's girlfriend. She was a city girl through and through.

Plus there was her career. Her last boyfriend had accused her of being married to her job. He'd meant it as an insult, but she hadn't taken it as such. Yes, she was dedicated to her work. It meant so much more to her than Simon with his penchant for Paisley jackets.

Their relationship hadn't lasted long after that and there'd been no one since. Her career and getting her doctorate meant everything to her; she didn't need the distraction of a relationship spoiling her chances of achieving her dream.

'Ooh, yes,' Gran agreed. 'Her dark to his blond would be stunning.'

'Gran!' hissed Ellie. 'Stop that now. Don't even think about it.'

'She does have beautiful eyes,' said

Jude, totally ignoring Ellie's outburst. 'They're such a deep, rich brown.'

'She has my son's eyes,' said Gran, 'and my daughter-in-law's lovely dark-skinned colouring. It's quite a stunning combination.'

Ellie shifted in her seat as Gran and Jude turned to peer at her.

Mercifully Tom re-entered the room and put a stop to the excruciating conversation. Whether his eyes were laughing because he'd heard what was said or whether this was his natural look, it was hard to tell. Ellie just hoped he'd been far enough away not to hear the bit about them being a lovely couple; she didn't want him to get any ideas either.

'I'll take a look at your fence, Mrs Potts, after I've helped clear up,' said Tom, as they finished their puddings.

'There's no need to help clear up,' said Ellie. 'I'll do it.'

Before anyone could argue she gathered up the empty bowls and took them into the kitchen.

★　★　★

From her position by the kitchen sink she could hear the sound of rumbling voices in the dining room. They continued for a few moments until the front door opened and closed and the house settled into a comfortable silence.

Ellie sank her hands into warm, soapy water and her shoulders relaxed. Gran's kitchen was, as always, deliciously cosy. Wooden beams stretched across the low ceiling and an old Welsh dresser was stacked with delicate china. A sofa took up one wall and Ellie remembered its colourful, squashy cushions as the most comfortable place in the house.

Through the window Ellie could see open fields disappearing down into the distance and the faint, twinkling blue of the sea at the edge of the horizon. There were cows grazing in the nearest field — Tom's, she supposed. Even as a girl who loved city living she could appreciate the scene's bucolic beauty.

She put the last plate in a cupboard with a satisfying clink and stepped back to admire her work. The kitchen was clear of the meal's detritus and the surfaces were shiny. A set of car keys rested in front of the kettle. Guessing they must be Jude's, Ellie picked them up and headed outside. Perhaps the bag had slipped under one of the seats and been missed in the struggle of getting Gran out of the car.

Ellie opened the driver's door and gave the interior a thorough search, but all she found was a chocolate wrapper and a car wash leaflet. A trip to town was looking increasingly likely.

She opened the boot and felt around the edges.

'Found any clues?' a deep voice, laced with laughter, said from behind her.

Ellie sighed and pulled at a thin piece of brown leather sticking out from the side of the boot lining. It gave way with a satisfying pop.

Triumphantly she turned round and held up a brown Burberry handbag for Tom to see. He was standing a little away from her, his shirt sleeves pushed back revealing muscular forearms. A fine line of sawdust had caught in the pale stubble along his jaw.

'I'm impressed,' he said. 'You've only been here two hours and you've already solved your first case.'

'Tom,' said Ellie frostily, 'what is it about me you find so amusing?'

Tom stopped smiling suddenly. He looked older without his customary grin.

'I don't find you funny,' he said quietly. 'I'm sorry if I've offended you in some way. That wasn't my intention.'

Ellie suddenly realised she was still holding the handbag aloft. She dropped it to her side, feeling ridiculous. Mum always said that for a person so observant in her work, she was a lost cause in social situations. Tom was being friendly and now she'd made him feel awkward. The chances of making a friend her age while she was here had slipped away.

'I . . . ' she began, not sure what to say next but feeling something was needed to fill the awkward silence developing.

'Ellie, Tom,' Jude called sharply from the front door, 'you'd best come quickly.'

Ellie forgot all about Tom and raced across the courtyard.

'What's wrong?' she choked out.

Had something worse happened to Gran? Had she fallen again? Was she conscious? Had the pain in her leg caused her to have a heart attack? Why was Ellie fussing about outside with a handbag when she should be with Gran, making sure she stayed safe?

Jude opened her mouth as if to speak but Ellie didn't stop to hear what she had to say. She raced inside, calling out to Gran.

She found her sitting in the lounge. The colour had leached out of her skin but otherwise she looked completely unharmed.

'What's wrong, Gran?' Ellie demanded.

'It's Andrew,' said Gran. 'All his cows have been stolen.'

This statement was so far removed from what she'd been expecting that Ellie could only blink at Gran. Above her Tom was firing questions but Ellie couldn't concentrate on the conversation. Her legs were trembling and she sank down onto the sofa.

She'd been so convinced Gran was about to die, and the reality didn't seem to be catching up with her body. Her heart was racing and her breathing wasn't getting enough oxygen into her lungs. If she didn't bring herself under control she was going to hyperventilate — which was a major overreaction to some missing cows.

She concentrated on pulling slow breaths into her lower lungs and breathing out through her lips. *It's only cows*, she repeated to herself, *only cows. Gran is fine.*

Slowly she calmed down and was able to look around her at everyone else. Gran was still deathly white. Her hands were wrapped tightly around the fabric of her skirt. Tom was standing at the window, his arms folded and his mouth set in a grim line. Jude was sitting in an armchair, her recently returned handbag on her lap, not looking as devastated as everyone else but still not the picture of happiness.

'Nobody's died,' reasoned Ellie. 'It's not as bad as all that.'

Gran said nothing; she started to fold the material of her skirt over and over again.

'It's devastating,' said Tom, his voice flat and cold.

'It's only cows,' protested Ellie.

Tom snorted and shook his head.

'Cow's are Andrew's life,' said Jude. 'His whole existence revolves around those animals.'

Ellie wrinkled her nose. Country folk were weird. She couldn't imagine giving more than a passing thought to a cow.

'Imagine,' said Tom, 'we were talking about someone's life savings. He loses his cows, he loses everything.'

Ah, that explained the grim faces. Ellie hadn't realised cows were such an investment. If pressed, she would have said one cow cost about the same as two hardback books.

How upsetting — poor Andrew, and how worrying for Tom if robbery on that scale was happening near his own livestock.

It didn't explain why Gran was so upset, though.

'Who's Andrew?' asked Ellie.

'My boyfriend,' said Gran.

3

Tom glanced in the rear view mirror to see Ellie intently studying the passing countryside. What was she thinking about behind her composed features?

He tried not to grin when he remembered last night and Ellie's reaction to Laura's revelation that Andrew was her boyfriend.

Even in the midst of the horrible news, Ellie's jaw-dropped incredulity had been amusing. It had even brought Laura round from her shocked state.

'Why are you looking like a fish, Ellie?' Laura had asked.

'*Boyfriend?*' Ellie had managed to croak.

'Well, I'm not going to call him my partner, am I? We're not in business together. And 'man friend' sounds ridiculous.'

It probably wasn't the name Ellie was

shocked about. Tom was pretty sure he'd feel shocked and mildly disorientated if his grandfather suddenly announced he had a girlfriend. Getting his head around that idea would be tough, and Ellie was probably feeling the same.

Tom had left Laura's house shortly after the boyfriend revelation but not before he'd promised to take Laura and Ellie to see Andrew the following morning. He had lots to do on the farm but in this small community, it was important to show solidarity with his fellow farmers. If livestock had been stolen from Andrew, then it could easily happen to him.

'Shall we stop for lunch at The Ship, Mrs Potts?' he asked, coming round to the present.

Laura had been badly shaken by their visit to Andrew's farm this morning and needed a treat, and Tom knew how she loved the food at The Ship. He was closer to Laura than his own maternal grandparents, who had been upset when his mum had married a farmer and were slightly disapproving of his choice to follow in his father's footsteps. They made their opinion very clear every time he paid them a visit.

Laura had always been abundantly supportive of him and it pained him to see her so pale and sad. Her leg was turned at a strange angle while she sat in the passenger seat. It had been the only way to get her safely into the car but it made him wince every time he caught sight of her.

'That would be lovely — thank you, Tom,' she said gratefully.

Tom pulled into The Ship's car park and into the closest space to the front door he could find.

'The Ship does the best food around here,' he told Ellie. 'You're in for a real treat.'

Ellie smiled politely and climbed out of the car.

She really hadn't warmed to him at all after their initial encounter, which was a shame because Tom thought she was quite lovely. If she allowed herself to relax around him she would be stunning, but she was holding him at arm's length and giving out very stern 'I'm not interested' vibes.

He wasn't sure whether it was him she wasn't keen on — she'd seemed to think he was laughing at her yesterday when he'd only been a bit nervous. Or perhaps it was men in general she wasn't interested in. Nevertheless there was something about Ellie that made Tom want to ruffle her perfect façade to see what lay beneath. No one could be that neat and composed all the way through.

Before Ellie's visit, Laura had told anyone who listened about her granddaughter and her glittering career, and how she was already sought after for her insights into criminal psychology. Laura had been beside herself with excitement when Ellie had been on the radio talking about a series of burglaries, and for weeks anyone who popped round to her house had to listen to it on catch-up.

Not that anyone minded; Laura was always helping people in the community and it hadn't put anyone out to listen to the five-minute segment. In fact, Laura's enthusiasm was catching. Ellie didn't know it but she was a bit of a local celebrity.

Perhaps Ellie's 'not interested' vibes were because she was a career woman with no interest in dating. Tom wasn't going to push it — there was no point flirting with a woman who wasn't interested. Besides, she was only around for a few weeks. There was no point starting something that couldn't be finished.

Ellie went to the back of the car and lifted out the wheelchair. Tom helped Laura out of her seat and then lowered her gently into the chair.

Inside, the pub was busy even though it was still early. Ellie found them a small table near the bar. After a few minutes of rearranging the furniture they were comfortably ensconced and

Tom passed round the menus.

It was strange to be around Laura when she wasn't bubbling over with enthusiasm. Even when she'd broken her leg she'd still been cheerful and full of laughter, but this morning had taken its toll. It was hard to be cheerful when faced with Andrew's utter desolation.

Andrew had taken them to see the barn from where the cows had been taken. The barn door had been hanging open with a broken padlock lying abandoned on the nearby grass. The large animal shelter had been devastatingly empty. It was one of the most depressing things Tom had ever seen, especially with the normally loquacious Andrew standing next to the broken door, drooping with sadness.

The thieves had known what they were doing. It wasn't easy to manoeuvre a large herd of cows onto a vehicle, and to do it at night would be extra hard. It couldn't have been done by one man, and whoever it was must have experience of handling livestock. That should narrow down the list of people responsible.

Tom glanced at his menu — not that he needed to look at it. He was having chicken and ham pie and chunky chips. He tried not to be boring and have this every time he came here, but it never failed to taste amazing — and Laura wasn't the only one who needed cheering up.

'What are you two having?' asked Tom. 'I'll go up and order.'

'I'll pay,' said Laura, digging into her large handbag and pulling out a battered purse.

After a few minutes of wrangling Laura won the right to pay — she was down but not out — and Tom went up to the bar to give their order.

He was setting the drinks on the table, a fruit juice each for him and Ellie and a glass of wine for Laura, when Laura said, 'So what do you think, then, Ellie?'

Ellie looked up over the rim of her glass and took a tiny sip of her drink.

'Erm . . . it's very nice,' she said tentatively.

Laura frowned.

'What is?' she asked.

'The juice,' Ellie clarified.

Tom took a sip from his drink to hide his smile. He knew where this was going; what was the point in having a criminal expert in the family if you couldn't ask them for advice when a crime occurred?

'I didn't mean the drink, darling. I meant what do you think about Andrew's situation?'

Ellie took a longer sip of her drink and then carefully set the glass down on the table.

'Well, it's obviously devastating for him. When do you think he'll get the money from the insurance company?'

Laura tutted in annoyance and took a large gulp of wine.

'They'll probably try to weasel out of paying him a thing. But that's also not what I meant. I was wondering what clues you noticed while we were there.

If we can find out who did it, maybe we can get the cows back before they're sold on or slaughtered.'

Ellie was saved from answering by the arrival of lunch. As always, the pie looked stunning. The puff pastry was golden. Tom used his fork to cut through the topping and was rewarded with the sight of chunky cuts of meat. He dug in.

After a few silent mouthfuls Ellie said, 'Gran, I didn't go there looking for clues. I went to support you and your . . . em, your . . . Andrew.'

'But you must have seen something,' Laura insisted.

Ellie popped a chip in her mouth and chewed slowly. Tom took a large mouthful of pie to stop himself from laughing out loud. Laura was as tenacious as usual. Ellie was going to have to up her game if she was going to compete with her grandmother.

'I didn't see anything other than what Andrew pointed out and what the local police already know,' said Ellie.

Laura opened her mouth but Ellie forestalled her by covering Laura's hand with one of her own.

'Gran, the police round here will know about local gangs who are capable of pulling off this sort of heist. I'm not going to annoy them by interfering in their investigation, especially as I'm an academic and not in law enforcement. Besides this sort of crime isn't my area of expertise.'

Laura opened her mouth again.

'It would be unprofessional,' said Ellie, before Laura could say anything.

That was a good card to play; Laura was very proud of Ellie's career and wouldn't want to do anything to jeopardise it. Still, Tom was disappointed when Laura closed her mouth and slumped back in her chair. She didn't normally back down from anything without protest.

He'd witnessed her persuading the almost reclusive vicar into hosting a cake sale to raise money for the local school. The cake sales were now a regular feature in Morwenna Bay's social calendar and had so far paid for an extensive climbing frame and an interactive white board.

Ellie and Laura lapsed into silence so Tom was grateful when Mike, The Ship's landlord, came over to chat to them.

'Laura,' said Mike, his cheerful voice booming over them all, 'it's wonderful to see you out and about. How's that leg of yours?'

'I'm doing very well, thank you, Mike. It won't be long before this cast can come off and then I'll be back to my dancing.'

Tom saw Ellie frown. Laura was being wildly optimistic. He hoped she was making polite conversation rather than truly believing she was going to get better so quickly. It was a very nasty break and once the cast was off there would be many months of physio-therapy before she could walk properly. Dancing could be years off, if she was ever able to again.

Laura turned to Ellie.

'This is my granddaughter, Ellie,' she said to Mike. 'She's come to stay with me while I recuperate. Ellie, do you remember Mike? His parents live in the white house on the corner. They're the Joneses — but not the Joneses who run the bakery. They're the Joneses who had the white dog . . . '

Ellie smiled politely at Mike, while Laura gave a summary of his family's work history and the various pets they'd had over the years.

Mike's brown curls sprang around his head as he nodded along to Laura's monologue, but he kept his eyes on Ellie's upturned face. Tom was fairly sure Ellie was giving off her normal not-interested vibes but Mike seemed to be entranced anyway.

'It's lovely to meet you, Ellie,' said Mike, when Laura had finished. 'You must come down and visit us on Friday evening. We're having a band and serving tapas. Your drinks are on the house to say welcome to the village. It's always good to have newcomers.'

Tom rolled his eyes. Yes, it was always good to have newcomers in the village. Most of the residents had been around forever, including him and Mike who'd been in school together. But Mike didn't go round offering drinks to everyone — his offer had more to do with Ellie's large brown eyes and long legs than welcoming a newcomer.

'You'll be here too, won't you, Tom?' said Mike, finally dragging his eyes away from Ellie.

'Sure, I wouldn't miss it.'

No offer of any free drinks. Tom caught his friend's eye; Mike grinned and winked. He knew Tom was on to him and he didn't care.

Tom grinned. Fair enough, but he suspected Mike wouldn't get anywhere.

'Can I get any of you pudding?' asked Mike.

'The cheesecake's particularly good.'

'Mike's always this modest,' Tom told Ellie and was rewarded with a genuine, warm smile from her.

'Of course we'll all have cheesecake,' said Laura. 'Make sure they're all large pieces.'

★ ★ ★

True to his word, Mike's cheesecake was sublime; a mixture of light vanilla topping on a rich, chocolate brownie base. By the time Tom was pulling up outside Laura's house he was swearing he would never eat again.

'Thank you so much for driving us about this morning, Tom,' said Laura. 'It was very kind of you. If I could trouble you with one more thing?'

'Of course,' said Tom. They made their way slowly into the house. Tom wasn't the only one showing the effects of all that food at lunchtime.

'What can I do for you?' he asked.

'In the spare room,' said Laura, 'at the end of the corridor is a large wooden box with engravings of elephants along one side. Would you be a dear and bring it into the lounge?'

Ellie shrugged; she had no idea what was going on either.

A large box matching Laura's description was at the foot of a single bed. Tom grabbed it by the handles on either end of the box and hefted it through to the lounge where Ellie had successfully assisted Laura onto the settee.

He put the box on the seat next to Laura and stepped back. He should be getting back to the farm. He had a million and one things to do . . . but he was curious. Where was this going?

Laura lifted the lid and started searching through the box, muttering to herself as she pushed various objects out of the way.

'Ah, here it is,' she said eventually and she pulled out an ancient cork board.

'What's that for?' asked Ellie, a hint of wariness in her voice.

'It's for our incident room.'

'Our what?' asked Ellie, confused.

'We'll need something to pin our

45

evidence to and somewhere to display our suspects,' Laura beamed in triumph.

'Gran, I — '

Suddenly Tom hoped Ellie would play along with this. Laura always had to be doing something and this would do no harm to the real investigation. They could talk about clues and suspects at home and no one would be any the wiser. It would help keep Laura entertained at a time when she needed it most.

Ellie must have followed the same train of thought because instead of arguing she took the board gently out of Laura's hands and placed it on top of the box, moving the whole thing along so she could sit next to Laura.

'Gran,' Ellie began softly taking one of Laura's hands in her own, 'we could do this and it might be a really interesting project for us both, but . . . what if we investigate and find an answer you don't like?'

'Don't be daft. If we solve the crime

I'd be thrilled, and so would Andrew.'

Ellie's lips tightened.

'But Gran — what if this is a case of fraud?'

'What are you saying, Ellie?'

'I'm saying what if the motivation is the money from the insurance claim? I'm saying, what if the person responsible is Andrew?'

4

Wood smoke scented the late evening air as Tom made a second tour of his outbuildings. When he'd taken over the farm from his parents he'd spent a lot of time improving and securing the barns by mending broken latches and patching up any holes, but this evening he wanted to check there was nothing he'd missed. Losing any livestock would be a disaster — one he couldn't afford. He'd be furious with himself if something happened when he could have easily prevented it.

As he made his way around, everything looked as secure as the last time he'd checked, but he still couldn't relax. He was going to have to get CCTV fitted; a depressingly costly but necessary evil.

Tilly skittered over to him as he came round the edge of the final barn and into the large courtyard that lay at the centre of his farm buildings. She nudged his leg searching for treats and he rubbed behind her ears absent-mindedly. Tilly was the sweetest Border collie he'd owned, with endless love for anyone she met. She'd make a useless guard dog. She'd probably lie down and wait for her tummy to be tickled as poachers made off with all his cattle.

Realising Tom wasn't hiding any treats in his pockets, Tilly settled down at his feet and he gazed out, past his outbuildings and beyond the fields towards the sea. Normally the soft roll of the water relaxed him but it didn't seem to be working its charm tonight.

'Hello,' said a familiar light-hearted voice.

'Mum,' said Tom in delight turning to see his mother approaching. 'What are you doing here?'

Tilly's tail went crazy, whipping back and forth and almost bending her body in half, she was so thrilled to see Tom's mum, Lynn. Tom leaned down slightly and kissed his mother's soft cheek, breathing in the familiar scent of her lavender soap. She looked as smart as always, with her grey hair neatly styled in a bob and she wore black leggings and a long aubergine jumper. The only scruffy thing about her was the thick mud covering her Hunter wellies. She'd obviously come over the fields to visit him.

'I heard about Andrew,' she said sadly as she slipped her arms around Tom's waist and gave him a quick squeeze. He squeezed her back and dropped a quick kiss on her forehead before letting go. Tilly leapt up to try and get involved and Tom pushed her gently down.

'Ah,' said Tom. 'It's bad, Mum. I went to see him today and he was broken. He's lost without his cattle.'

They looked at each other in quiet contemplation — they both understood Andrew's pain. Lynn broke the silence.

'I've walked up to see how you're

doing in light of the break-in. I know you must be worried.'

'I've bought a padlock and chain. I'm going to attach it to the gate tonight. If someone tries to come through it, I should wake up. I'm going to get CCTV tomorrow, which I've resisted up until now but I think I'll need it for peace of mind.'

'Just promise me you won't try tackling anyone who tries to get through on your own,' said Lynn.

'Don't worry, I'm not into heroics. I'm not going to get into a fight with a potentially armed gang.'

'I know you wouldn't intentionally get into a fight, but I worry about your safety,' said Lynn anxiously. 'You're isolated up here.'

'I know you worry.' Tom slung an arm around his mum's thin shoulders. 'But if you and Dad were still here it wouldn't matter if you were only dressed in your pyjamas, you'd be chasing after anyone if you thought they were after your cattle.'

'Too right. And if the sight of us half-dressed doesn't frighten them off, then nothing will.'

Tom chuckled. 'Are you coming in for a glass of wine?' he asked.

'Go on then. Your dad can make dinner.'

They made their way to the farmhouse, Tilly's tail thumping them as she walked between them.

'Dad and I heard from Roger Weekes yesterday,' Lynn said as they stepped into the kitchen and she started to pull off her boots.

'I haven't seen him since the mart at Haverfordwest back in March, which is crazy considering how close he lives,' said Tom as he opened the fridge door. He pulled out a bottle of wine and asked, 'How's he doing?'

'He's not so good. Half his stock was stolen from him last week.'

Tom froze as he reached for two glasses.

'You're kidding,' he said.

'I'm afraid not. As at Andrew's it

happened at night, and there is no clue as to who did it.'

Tom shook his head and poured his mum a glass of wine. He opened a beer for himself.

'Thanks,' she murmured, taking a large sip.

'Poor Roger,' Tom said, looking back out into his courtyard and shuddering.

Tom definitely wouldn't be getting much sleep tonight. Tomorrow he'd organise the CCTV. What a shame it had come to this. Morwenna Bay was known for its tranquillity and lack of crime. People often joked that the only crime round here was when Tom, aged sixteen, fell into the duck pond during a summer fair and accidentally knocked the nose off one of the surrounding statues. People still ragged him about it, calling it a case of criminal damage, but no one took it seriously. Until recently, that was the only crime anyone ever mentioned.

Tom had grown up in a village where people didn't lock their homes if they went out — and yet here he was, buying a heavy chain to secure his gates.

'How's Laura?' asked Lynn, breaking into his thoughts.

'She's still in a lot of discomfort with that leg but she's acting as if it's no big deal. She's taken Andrew's news badly, though.'

'She must be pleased that her Ellie has come to stay,' Lynn commented.

'She's thrilled.' Tom smiled and took a long cool glug of his beer.

'Ellie was a lovely child,' Lynn said, looking at him through narrowed eyes.

Tom smiled slightly. Obviously his mum had noticed just how lovely Tom had found Ellie when they were teenagers. She'd been like an exotic creature thrust into their midst and Tom had found her fascinating. The feeling hadn't been mutual.

He hadn't thought about her much since she'd stopped coming to visit her grandparents, but when he'd found her waiting for him at the bus station yesterday, he'd been struck again by her otherworldliness. She didn't belong in this tiny village.

'She's still pleasant,' said Tom cautiously.

His parents were keen for him to settle down and he didn't want them getting any ideas about Ellie. It was never going to happen.

'But she seems a bit uptight,' he added.

'Really? I'm surprised. She was an inquisitive, bright child. I remember how much she loved the animals. Didn't she try to smuggle one of the sheepdog puppies home in her coat pocket once? You should take Tilly over to see her. Tilly would make anyone unwind.'

Tom decided to ignore this last comment. It wasn't up to him to make Ellie relax and he didn't think she'd appreciate it if he tried. He didn't seem to have made a great first impression on her and things hadn't improved much since. He'd obviously annoyed her with his teasing, even though his intention had been to see if he could make her smile. He was going to let Ellie and her gran to get on with things without him from now on. He had enough to worry about.

He gestured to his mum to head through to the lounge and take a seat. The room faced out towards the sea. Last year he had installed floor-to-ceiling windows along one wall so that he had a panoramic view of his fields and the cliffs. He considered this one of his better ideas, even though he was still paying for the alteration.

They sat and watched the distant sea undulating gently for a moment, both lost in their own thoughts.

'Laura seems to think Ellie can use her academic skills to solve the mystery as to who's taken Andrew's cows,' Tom told his mum eventually. 'She's set up her own incident room in her dining room. When I left yesterday afternoon it consisted of a pinboard with a pencil drawing of their only suspect. Knowing Laura, there's a whole police team working in there now.'

Lynn laughed. 'Typical Laura. She just can't sit still and wait for things to be done, she has to get stuck in herself. Who's the suspect?'

'I'd better not tell you,' said Tom.

Tom didn't think Laura would appreciate him spreading the rumour that Andrew might be guilty. He recalled her indignation at Ellie's suggestion. In the end, she had conceded that Andrew had to be considered, if only so that he could be found innocent. The police and the insurance company would certainly be investigating him, so Laura believed she and Ellie could prove his innocence while also tracking down the real culprits.

'If he's not already a suspect, then Laura should add Simon Hawley to her pinboard,' said Lynn. 'He's out of prison.'

Tom snorted. Neither he nor his mum was a fan of Simon's. In fact very few people locally were.

'Surely he wouldn't go straight out and commit the same crime he was put away for?' asked Tom sceptically. 'That would be madness.'

'If he's stolen cattle before then he'll probably do it again. Maybe he learned some clever new techniques in prison and is hoping he won't get caught this time. He must be the police's prime suspect. You should ring Laura and let her know.'

Ellie's point — that the local police were good people who wouldn't want amateurs like Laura and him bumbling around potentially meddling with evidence — was a good one.

He pictured Laura with her broken leg, and the way she always carried on, smiling and trying to make everyone around her happy. And he pictured her yesterday, so sad and broken.

He'd ring her and let her know about Simon Hawley. What harm could it do?

5

'Remind me again why we're doing this?' asked Ellie.

'Because your gran asked us and the indomitable Mrs Potts is impossible to refuse,' replied Tom, grinning.

Ellie tapped her fingers on the Volvo's glove compartment as Tom drove through narrow country lanes. Tom was right; Gran was incredibly enthusiastic about solving the case of the missing cows. As soon as Tom had rung two days ago to tell them about Roger's sheep and the possible Simon Hawley connection, Gran had started planning her next move and, as Ellie had watched her sparkle of excitement grow at a new development, she'd felt the enthusiasm sweep her along too. It would be great if they could find some evidence that proved, beyond a doubt, that Andrew wasn't involved in the disappearance of his own livestock.

Together Ellie and Gran had devised some questions for Roger, but this morning Gran had been in too much pain to get in Tom's car and so they'd gone without her.

Without Gran, Ellie was a little nervous. What if Roger and Mary thought they were wasting their time answering her questions when she wasn't the police?

A panting head appeared by Ellie's shoulder. When Ellie had met Tilly earlier, it had been love at first sight for both of them. She knew Tom wouldn't be parted from Tilly and that there was no place for a dog in her busy work schedule, but that didn't stop Ellie from imagining long Sunday afternoons walking Tilly through the large open spaces of Regent's Park. She reached up and tickled the collie under her chin and received a few loving licks in return.

'You'd best tell me exactly what happened to Roger,' said Ellie. 'Gran's so convinced his sheep have been stolen by the same person who took Andrew's cows, and that this person is probably Simon Hawley, that she's not really allowing for the fact that he might be innocent.'

Tom changed gear and the car slowed as he followed a tight bend in the road.

'Roger's been breeding sheep for twenty years,' he said when the road straightened out. 'He's well-known and well-respected. His sheep graze on the salt marches of the Bargoed estuary, which give the meat a distinct salty flavour.'

'Isn't that dangerous? Don't the sheep get washed away by the tide?' Ellie asked, alarmed.

Tom's eyes sparkled with amusement.

'No, they don't. I don't know if you know this being a city girl, but sheep have eyes and legs. They can see the water coming and move out of the way as it approaches.'

'Ha,' said Ellie, 'very funny,' but she was smiling at his gentle teasing. She was starting to enjoy his jokey banter now that she was getting used to it.

'It's hard to get to Roger's sheep. They're out quite far when the tide is out and they're close to his farm when it's in. The only access to them at that point is through Roger's farm. They were in the barn last Wednesday for a vaccination but they'd been split between two barns, which was lucky or he'd probably have lost the lot. At some point during the night one half was taken.'

Ellie reached into her handbag and pulled out a battered notebook. Gran would question her intently when she got back, so she'd better make some notes. She rested the book on her knees and scribbled down a few points.

'Where does this Simon Hawley fit in?' she asked when she'd finished writing.

'A few years ago, Simon and his gang rustled some sheep over in the next county. It wasn't long before he was caught and he spent some time in jail. He's well-known around here as a petty criminal and I'm sure the police will be looking into him. My parents are pretty certain Simon's involved, but I'm not so sure. These two crimes have required a degree of sophistication and forward planning. I'm not convinced Simon has the ability. All the crimes of his that I know about have an opportunistic quality to them.'

Ellie made another note in her book. The Volvo crested a hill and the wide panorama of the estuary opened up in front of them. The tide was out and a thin river cut through low-lying marshland, shining like an opal under the bright summer sun.

'Wow,' said Ellie, 'it's beautiful.'

'Yes it is,' said Tom pulling into a lay-by and slowing to a stop. 'You see that white house and the other side of the river to the left of the bridge?'

'Yes.'

'That's Roger's farmhouse. The

sheep roam all over the lowlands you can see during the low tide.'

'I can't see any sheep out now.'

'No,' said Tom grimly. 'He's got them in a field at the moment, but his unique selling point is the salty flavour of the meat. There are only two other places in the whole of the UK which have the same claim as him so as you can imagine he's very passionate about what he does. He's not going to get the distinct flavour from the grass in the field. It's not a long-term solution.'

'He should be OK with them out roaming during the day,' said Ellie. 'I can't see how anyone would be able to round them up and get them into a lorry from here without people seeing for miles around.'

The valley was overlooked as far as the eye could see on both sides. Houses dotted the landscape, sometimes alone and sometimes in clusters. There would be thousands of witnesses on both sides of the estuary to a daytime theft.

'I know, but he's spooked. He's

already lost so much. He doesn't want to lose any more.'

Ellie nodded and made some more notes. She had a lot of information but no tangible evidence.

Tom pulled out of the lay-by and headed down towards the river through twisted country lanes.

'How do you want to handle this morning?' asked Tom.

Ellie let out a long breath.

'I don't know what Gran told Roger on the phone. I was in the shower at the time she spoke to him. I have a horrible feeling she's promised him we will solve the case this afternoon. I really don't want to get his hopes up because realistically I don't see what you and I can do.'

Tom nodded. 'It is possible she told him that we'll help to solve the case. She is very proud of you and probably thinks you can do it all by yourself.'

Ellie groaned. 'I know, but . . . '

The truth was, it would be interesting to try and solve the mystery. She'd love to be able to help but she was worried she wouldn't be able to give it her full attention with everything else she had on. She didn't want to get anyone's hopes up and then disappoint when she'd found nothing out before she had to return to London.

Then again, the investigation had already proved to be a good thing to chat to Gran about whenever they were alone together. Gran needed something to take her mind off her reduced mobility and this was proving to be a great distraction. If Ellie could find enough clues for them to ponder over together, it would continue to give Gran something to concentrate on.

'I think,' Tom said, breaking into her thoughts, 'that Roger will be grateful for our support and appreciate us going to his farm just to listen to what he has to say. If one of us says something that triggers a helpful thought then that's a bonus.

'Plus,' he added as he eased onto the bridge across the estuary, 'us going will make Laura happy and she needs cheering up.'

'That's true,' said Ellie. 'Do you know she Googled Simon Hawley's image so she could draw a likeness for her pinboard? She remembered what he looked like as a teenager but apparently that wasn't good enough for the board.'

'She's a good artist,' said Tom, amused.

'Hmm,' murmured Ellie, distracted by their arrival at Roger's farm.

The gates to the farmyard were open. Weeds wound their way around the bottom slats. They must remain permanently open. Hardly a robust defence!

Tom drove down a long, curving driveway, which was also showing signs of neglect with parts of abandoned machinery lying along the sides and weeds running rampant. Tom slowed slightly as they passed a large dilapidated barn.

'This is where the sheep were taken from. As you can see, its entrance is hidden from the house. It would have made taking the sheep easier than taking the cattle at Andrew's farm where the barn is in full view of the farmhouse.'

'Can you stop the car?' asked Ellie.

'Sure.'

Tom stopped and Ellie hopped out. She walked towards the barn door, which was padlocked by a brand new, unwieldy-looking lock. She could clearly see where the previous lock had been forced open, although judging by the rust on the mechanism it wouldn't have taken a great deal of effort to open it. The grass up to the door was flattened, which suggested the barn was well-used, but on either side of the door weeds continued to grow in abundance.

It terms of upkeep Roger's farm was a world away from Andrew's meticulously neat grounds. They also specialised in different livestock, yet they'd both been targets for theft.

'The two farms and their livestock are very different,' Ellie called out to

Tom. 'Is there anything that connects the two of them?'

Tom leaned over so Ellie could see him. 'They're friends and have both worked in the area for many years but I can't think of anything that connects them more specifically than to any of us farmers around here.'

She climbed back into the car and made some more notes in her book. Nothing she'd written so far helped, but hopefully some of it would come in useful later.

'I know Roger's farm doesn't look great,' said Tom as he continued driving, 'but he's very strict about animal welfare. Inside the barn, the conditions are good; he just doesn't spend money on making his farm look pretty.'

Ellie nodded. 'I can see that.'

Tom drove on and they arrived in a wide courtyard. Tom pulled up outside a large, grey stone farmhouse and turned off the engine.

'Ready?' he asked.

'Yes,' she said, hoping that Roger and Mary wouldn't view her visit as a waste of time and that she would be able to think of something not just to prove Andrew's innocence, but also to help them. Even a tiny clue would be great.

They stepped out of the car and Tom rapped loudly on the front door.

A short, stocky man with dark hair and wild eyebrows answered. Although his weathered face was etched with laughter lines, he wasn't smiling today. Gran had told Ellie she'd met Roger and Mary when she was little, but she had no recollection of the man standing before her.

'Hi, Roger,' said Tom gently. 'How are you doing?'

'I've been better, Tom,' said Roger. 'Hello, Ellie, I don't suppose you remember me. You were a tiny girl last time I met you. Laura keeps Mary and me updated on your progress. She's so proud of how well you're doing.'

Ellie stepped forward and shook Roger's hand warmly; the skin of his hand was rough.

'I'm so sorry for your loss, Roger,' she said. 'May we come in so you can tell us all about it?'

'Of course, please come through to the lounge.'

Ellie, Tom and Tilly followed Roger through a narrow hallway lined with family photographs. The lounge was dark and cosy with every available space covered in trinkets or overflowing piles of paper. Roger pushed a large ginger cat aside, which didn't wake as it was slid across, and sat down on a threadbare armchair. Tom and Ellie took the settee and Tilly settled by their feet, unbothered by the slumbering feline.

'Mary will bring us through some tea and hopefully some scones,' said Roger. 'It's been hours since breakfast.'

As if to illustrate his point his stomach rumbled loudly and he laughed, bringing some life back into his face.

As Roger told them what had

71

happened, Mary joined them with the promised tea and cake. The scones were still warm and Ellie managed to spread hers liberally with thick, salty butter and strawberry jam as Roger talked.

Most of what he said was what Ellie had already heard from Laura and Tom; only Roger went into much more detail about the sheep. He stocked Badger Face Welsh Mountain sheep, which was a breed Ellie knew nothing about. Until the beginning of this conversation she had just assumed that sheep were either black or white but Roger's were white with a thick black stripe running from their necks down across their bellies. Roger told her all about their breeding habits and the general hardiness of the animal.

It was more detail than Ellie really needed to know and would mostly forget. What she did get from Roger was that these weren't just sheep to Roger and Mary. They were part of their family. Roger had been at the birth of all of them. He had watched over them as they'd grown, and cared for them deeply. It wasn't just about the money; it was a personal loss as well.

'It sounds as if you rarely bring the sheep in from the estuary,' said Ellie as Roger finished talking and helped himself to another scone.

'That's right,' he said. 'Only if there's a storm coming or they need checking over by the vet or, of course, when they're off to market. Otherwise they're free to roam.'

'Who would know that you were bringing them in on that particular day?'

'The police asked me that and the truth is, lots of people knew the sheep were coming in that day. It's such a rare occurrence I'd have talked about it with friends and fellow farmers and the vet, obviously. But as you can see, the marshlands are overlooked by thousands of homes. Anyone could have been watching me herding up the sheep and bringing them in. Even if they hadn't seen it happening, anyone in those houses would have noticed the sheep weren't out on the marshes as normal.'

'Does the vet . . . ?'

'You can count her out as a suspect,' said Roger straight away. 'Not only is she as straight as they come but she also has an alibi for the night. She was over in Bristol giving a talk at some swanky dinner. It's not her.'

Ellie nodded and made a note in her pad. Just because the vet was away didn't rule her out as an accomplice but it did lessen the likelihood of her involvement. She'd have to check whether Andrew had the same vet.

Then, of course, there was everyone who worked with the vet and anyone she may have visited and discussed her schedule. It was a mountain of people. Ellie was only here for another three and a half weeks. Even Sherlock Holmes couldn't get through all those people in that time.

'What was the latest time you know that the sheep were in the barn?' asked

Ellie showing no outward sign of her despondency.

'I checked on them before I called it a night. I'd been to The Ship for a pint so I was later than usual. I'd say it was around ten-thirty.'

'Did you hear anything unusual in the night?'

Roger sighed and shook his head.

'I don't sleep well and I'd taken some tablets to help. I was out of it, I'm afraid.'

Ellie turned to Mary.

'I wear earplugs — he snores,' she said.

'That's not true,' protested Roger his face crinkling in indignant amusement. 'I breathe heavily at most.'

'He snorts like a pig,' Mary mock-whispered to Ellie.

Ellie giggled. She liked this couple and wished there was more she could do to help them.

'Gran mentioned someone called Simon Hawley. It seems he's got a history of committing this sort of crime. Do you know him?'

Roger snorted, 'Everyone knows Simon. He's not just got a 'history of committing this sort of crime' — he's got a history of crime, full stop.'

'We knew him when he was younger,' said Mary sadly.

'Aye,' said Roger. 'When he was a teenager the powers that be still had some hope of rehabilitating him. He did some community work at our farm. He was here about a month.'

'He could be very charming,' said Mary.

'Yes — he was charm itself until he made off with some of our china,' said Roger gloomily.

'We never did get that back,' said Mary. 'Still, it wasn't worth very much so goodness knows what he did with it.'

'Tom mentioned that he was an opportunistic thief. Would you agree with that assessment?'

'He was when he was younger,' said Mary. 'I'd put the china on the kitchen table to give the cabinet a spring clean.

He'd never have seen it before because we didn't allow any of the lads into the lounge where it was normally kept. He saw it and took it and that was the last we saw of him.'

'He's had plenty of time to perfect the art of stealing,' said Roger bitterly.

Mary brought in more tea and another round of scones. Tom and Ellie stayed a while longer chatting about general things while enjoying Mary's home baking. Tom was making subtle moves to leave when Ellie thought of one more thing to ask.

'What do you think will happen to your missing stock?' she asked.

Roger's mood instantly darkened.

'Most likely they will be taken to an abattoir and slaughtered. Those crooks will then sell the meat, getting all that money without any of the hard work.'

'I don't know how it works,' said Ellie, 'but wouldn't a person with livestock asking for them to be slaughtered need to prove ownership first?'

'My sheep are all chipped so an

abattoir would know instantly they belong to me and not anyone else. But if you're given a hefty backhander to overlook the chips, well . . . '

'And what about selling the meat on? I heard on the radio that when meat is sold the buyer needs to know exactly where it's come from and that's supposed to be displayed on the packaging.'

'If you're a reputable supermarket then, yes, you would definitely want to know where your meat was coming from,' Mary agreed.

'Sadly it's not just supermarkets that sell meat. Not all vendors are reputable,' said Roger.

Ellie wanted to give him a big hug, she liked this stocky, garrulous man, but she settled on looking at him sympathetically.

Tom got to his feet and announced that he needed to get back to his farm. It was a lengthy goodbye with promises to return and bring Laura next time they visited but finally he, Ellie and

Tilly climbed back into the Volvo.

They drove in silence as Tom pulled out of the driveway and headed towards the bridge. Ellie looked over her copious notes, but nothing jumped out at her as important.

'You were great today,' said Tom, unexpectedly serious.

Tilly lent her judgement by poking her head between the seats and licking Ellie's face.

'Thanks, but I don't think I did anything. The whole situation is just incredibly frustrating.'

'You allowed them to talk and you took them seriously. That was enough. I could tell their spirits were lifted just by you being there.'

'It's not enough though, is it really?' Ellie said, sadness making her voice sound gruff. 'I'm not going to be able to return Roger's and Andrew's live-stock to them even if by some miracle I worked out who took the cattle right this minute. Their lives have changed completely and whatever the outcome of our or the police's investigation there's nothing anyone can do about that.'

6

Ellie cleared her throat and stared out at the fifteen women looking back at her. How had she got herself into this position?

When she'd been a student, ten years ago, she'd taken self-defence classes. She'd loved it and had raved about it to Gran whenever they'd chatted on the phone. But, and this was a big but, she'd stopped after a couple of years and moved onto Pilates. Since then there'd been tai chi, Zumba and a brief, painful period when she'd tried circuit training.

She'd been putting the breakfast dishes into the dishwasher earlier when Gran had said, 'I've had a really good idea, love.'

Ellie had been concentrating completely on removing the remains of muesli which had bonded with the bowls until she heard Gran saying, 'I know you love it so I told Jude, and she thought it was a fabulous idea and that we should all know about it because you can never be too safe. So what do you think?'

'Sorry, I wasn't listening. What do I love?' Ellie had asked, turning off the tap and slotting the bowls into the dishwasher.

'Self-defence classes.'

'Oh, yes, you're right, I used to love those. What about them?'

'Would you mind passing on your skills to some of the ladies?' Gran had asked.

'Of course,' Ellie had said, wiping down the surfaces. 'It would be my pleasure.'

Ellie had thought she'd be sitting in a pub telling a few of Gran's close friends about the manoeuvres she could remember. She hadn't realised Gran had been talking about giving a demonstration. By the time she'd realised they were talking about slightly different things the Community Hall had been booked and Gran was practically bouncing up and down in her chair with the excitement of showing off her granddaughter. Not wanting to disappoint anyone, Ellie had rushed into her room and had spent an hour researching self-defence techniques and practising the moves in the mirror.

That was how she now found herself, early in the evening, standing at the front of the Morwenna Bay Community Hall with all these women staring back at her expectantly. She took a deep breath and was rewarded with a lungful of dusty air, which didn't have the calming effect she'd intended.

Ellie glanced at Gran; she was alternating between beaming with pride and writing things down in a notebook. Ellie didn't know what was being written about but she had a feeling she would find out later and that finding out would involve the two of them sitting down in Gran's makeshift incident room to discuss clues.

Ellie smiled to herself. She hoped Gran was having more luck than she was. Since she'd visited Roger five days ago neither she nor Tom had come up with anything new. The thief hadn't struck again either, so there were no new clues to follow. On the upside, it had meant she'd had some time to start her thesis, which was positive even if she didn't like what she'd written so far.

Ellie cleared her throat again; she had best get started.

'OK, everyone, before we start with any movements I'm going to go over some basics. The best way to stay safe is not to put yourself in harm's way, so . . . '

Ellie chatted for five minutes and then demonstrated some simple moves, all the while silently thanking YouTube for her afternoon's research.

After half an hour she felt she'd done enough and she brought the session to a close. The Lavender Ladies broke into a spontaneous round of applause and

Ellie felt tears of relief spark her eyes. She glanced across. If it were possible to burst with pride, then Gran would be in pieces.

Ellie felt her heart swell. She was so glad she'd done the demonstration. It had given Gran so much joy and cost her nothing. Smiling, she made her way over to Gran who was surrounded by her friends, all congratulating her on producing such a clever granddaughter.

'We all go to the pub now, Ellie,' Gran told her when there was a pause in the conversation.

'Great,' said Ellie who was seriously looking forward to a large glass of prosecco or two. Even though the evening had gone well so far, her stomach still felt fluttery with nerves.

She unlocked the wheels of Gran's wheelchair and pushed her through the double doors of the community hall. Having done a lot of talking over the last half hour, she was content to let the women's chatter wash over her as they all made their way down the hill towards The Ship, whose gardens overlooked the bay.

⋆ ⋆ ⋆

Ellie hadn't taken much notice of the outside of The Ship the last time she'd visited. Tom had pulled up right outside the front door in the disabled spot so they could get Gran's wheelchair out of his car. Tonight she got a good look at the building as they made their way slowly towards it. It had certainly improved a lot since she was a child, when the pub had been popular due to its location and not on account of its peeling paint and uneven flagstones. Now, a low wall surrounded a large beer garden, which faced the sea. The garden was pretty, with flowers running over every available space. A large climbing frame stood in one corner and was covered in young children as their parents enjoyed a drink in the sunny evening air. Mike had added a long conservatory to the back of the pub and the doors were flung wide open. A steady stream of people passed in and out with drinks and food.

The Ship was packed with people inside as well but an area against the far wall had been kept aside for the Lavender Ladies. The group made sure there was enough space for Gran's chair before seating themselves. Ellie settled herself in a corner between the wall and Gran's chair. Jude sat on the other side of Gran and the two of them gabbled on about nothing in particular. Ellie was content to watch them and relax.

As soon as they were all seated, Mike and a barmaid appeared carrying large trays of prosecco and clinking champagne glasses.

'We ordered ahead,' Gran told Ellie as Mike opened the bottles and proceeded to pour generous measures.

'Good idea,' said Ellie as she was handed a tall glass filled with prosecco. She took a large gulp and revelled in the delicious bubbles popping on her tongue. As she swallowed, the knots in her back slowly eased.

Mike returned to the table with large wicker baskets, lined with fake newspaper and overflowing with chips. The baskets were quickly passed around the table.

'I wouldn't have made dinner if I'd known we were getting all this,' said Ellie.

'Ah, there's always room for chips,' said Gran as she leaned forward and grabbed a handful.

Feeling she'd earned it, Ellie snatched a few for herself before the basket in front of her was emptied. The chips were fat and crunchy and covered in a light dusting of salt. Maybe she should order some more baskets because it turned out there was plenty of room for these moreish chips, as all the other members of the group were demonstrating. Within minutes all the baskets were empty.

'Ellie,' said Gran breaking into her thoughts. 'Have you met Charlotte yet?'

Ellie glanced up to see a young

woman standing next to Gran's shoulder. Ellie stood up to shake her hand and was confronted with the most beautiful woman she'd ever seen. Long blonde hair fell to Charlotte's tiny waist. Her pale skin was smooth and her full pink lips curved into a natural smile.

'No,' said Ellie, 'we've not been introduced but I think I saw you at the back of the hall earlier.'

Charlotte was hard to miss.

'That was me,' said Charlotte taking Ellie's proffered hand and shaking it warmly. 'Your class was great fun. Will you be doing another one soon?'

'I don't think so,' said Ellie at the same time as Gran said, 'Yes, definitely.'

'Well, maybe,' said Ellie, smiling at Gran's enthusiasm.

'That's fantastic!' said Charlotte. 'I'll look forward to it. I'm going to practise my kicking in front of the mirror tonight.'

Charlotte demonstrated her defensive kick and Ellie hoped the girl would never need to use that particular move.

It wouldn't do her any good. Ellie focused very hard on not smiling but the large glass of prosecco she'd already finished made it very difficult to maintain her composure. She glanced at Gran who also seemed to be trying to hide a smile.

Ellie dipped her head and studied the floor. Charlotte seemed very sweet and she didn't want to upset her by laughing at her. Perhaps Gran was right; more self-defence classes were needed. Ellie didn't think she was a great teacher but it was fair to say she was better at self-defence than the beautiful Charlotte.

'Charlotte has some exciting news,' said Gran, breaking into Ellie's thoughts.

'Oh?' said Ellie politely.

'I got engaged at the weekend.' Charlotte shimmered with pleasure.

'Congratulations, that's lovely news,' said Ellie, suspicious as to where this line of conversation was going.

'Show Ellie your gorgeous ring,' Gran insisted.

As Charlotte held out her left hand to show the large diamond on her ring finger Gran sent Ellie a significant look. Ellie tried to ignore it as she made what she hoped were appropriate cooing noises. Ellie wasn't really one for jewellery, she would rather have a fabulous pair of boots, but she recognised that this was a serious ring. Why Gran thought that was significant she didn't know, but she was confident Gran would tell her before the evening was out.

Ellie hadn't needed to worry about buying more chips. No sooner had the baskets emptied than they were whisked away and replaced by more. At some point, trays of pitta bread with olives and houmous arrived too.

The conversation moved from engagements to weddings, buying houses and to babies. Several conversations ran on at the same time and bursts of laughter erupted every few minutes. Ellie felt the warmth of the friendship group wash over her. She didn't really have anything like this in her real life. She was too busy working to spend much time with friends; she ought to make more effort to catch up with the girls she'd lived with at university. She realised that she missed the banter and support only a large group of friendly women could provide.

At the end of her second glass of prosecco Ellie decided she needed an apple juice. She had to push Gran up a substantial hill if they were to make it home later and she didn't want to run her into a ditch because she'd had one too many! She squeezed out of her narrow space and made her way to the bar.

The crowds from earlier had thinned out and only a handful of customers were dotted around the pub. Mike was deep in conversation with a portly gentleman. Ellie had had enough alcohol not too worry too much about interrupting.

'Hi Mike,' she called cheerfully.

'Ellie,' said Mike grinning as he made

his way towards her. 'It's lovely to see you again. I was hoping you'd come in with the Lavender Ladies. I missed you at the tapas night.'

'I'm sorry I wasn't able to come,' said Ellie. 'I've been working really hard to establish how I can best help Gran and what I absolutely mustn't do to take away her independence.'

'Of course, it must be hard for you both. Don't worry, I was only teasing about tapas night although I hope you will come along to our next one this Friday. The promise of free drinks still stands.'

'Thanks, Mike. I'll look forward to it.'

The two glasses of prosecco had relaxed Ellie to the point that the thought of turning up at a pub on her own where she didn't know anyone didn't seem to be bothering her.

'Do you have bands playing often?' she asked.

'It's a new thing I'm trying to introduce. I get a lot of business, being one of the two pubs in the village, but the brewery have just put the rents up so I'm trying out new things to draw in more customers. The bands seem to be a huge success so I'm going to try and keep that going. I've had less success with other initiatives I've tried out. The less said about my date night idea, the better.'

Mike pulled a face of disgust and Ellie laughed.

'Sorry, Ellie, I can see Bob trying to get my attention. Can I get you a drink before I go and see what he wants?' Mike asked.

She ordered a fruit juice and watched as Mike stretched to open the fridge door behind him.

'Wow,' she said as she spotted the intricate design on his forearm, 'that's an impressive tattoo.'

'Thanks,' he said holding his arm out and rolling back his sleeve for her to get a better look. 'It's a Celtic knot. I was planning on having a thick band around my bicep but the tattooist talked me into getting my whole forearm done. You should have been there the day my mum spotted it. She hit the roof, but I think it's grown on her. She's stopped tutting whenever she sees it, at any rate.'

'It's stunning,' said Ellie, lightly tracing the elaborate loops and curves on his arm.

'Thanks,' he said shyly.

Ellie glanced up and noticed his cheeks had turned a little pink. She realised that she was, to all intents and purposes, stroking his arm and she jerked her hand back.

'Sorry,' she said. 'It looks so real I forgot it was part of you.'

He laughed and said, 'I'm not going to complain if a beautiful girl touches my arm. Now, if you'll excuse me I think Bob is getting very thirsty.'

Mike smiled and disappeared to the other end of the bar.

Ellie picked up her drink and was just about to return to her table when she spotted Tom and Andrew enjoying a quiet pint together.

Ellie had disliked Andrew when she'd first met him. She'd taken one look at his slim frame and made the snap decision that he was too different from her Grandad, whose delicious chunkiness she'd love to cuddle, so she was never going to warm to him. She was grown up enough to realise that her judgement had been based on her own feelings of resentment of him taking her grandfather's place rather than on anything he'd said or done. It wasn't his fault her wonderful Grandad was no longer alive and she couldn't blame Gran for finding happiness with somebody else. Life was too short.

Before she thought about it too much, Ellie made her way over to the two men. She owed it to her gran to make Andrew feel welcome into their family. She would try and approach him without comparing him to Grandad. That he was sitting next to the increasingly attractive Tom had nothing to do with her decision.

'Ellie,' said Tom, spotting her before she reached the table. 'Come and join us.'

He pushed out a spare chair and Ellie smiled at him gratefully.

'I came over to see whether there's any new information on your missing cows, Andrew,' Ellie said as she sat down.

Andrew shook his thin head sadly.

'They've disappeared without a trace,' he said. 'I've no hope they'll be found now.'

Ellie nodded, feeling inadequate in the face of his grief. Just as she'd found when trying to comfort Roger, there was nothing she could say to make him feel better. Andrew drew a deep breath and physically pulled himself upright.

'Did you enjoy your first evening with the Lavender Ladies?' he asked politely.

'Yes,' said Ellie grateful to be moving on to a more cheerful topic and impressed with how Andrew had managed to pull himself together. Her mother would call him a true gentle-man.

Ellie was coming round to the idea that Andrew wasn't guilty of fraud. She hadn't found any solid evidence to support her feelings and she really hoped something would come to light soon which would provide the proof she needed.

She made Tom and Andrew laugh with her description of the self-defence lesson and how she'd been frantically researching what to do on YouTube. Without the weight of his loss pressing down on him Andrew became more animated and Ellie could see what had attracted her gran to him. His ability to spin an amusing anecdote reminded her a little of Grandad, so they weren't as different as she'd first thought.

She mustn't let her own grief colour her judgement of the man. She would try, in future, to be more open-minded when she met up with him. Unless, of course, he really was guilty of fraud — and then Ellie would never forgive him for upsetting Gran.

Andrew finished his pint and stood up.

'I'm going to say goodnight to Laura and then head home. Thanks for bringing me out tonight, Tom. I needed to stop moping around the house and this evening has been good for me. It's been lovely to talk to you properly too, Ellie.'

'I'm glad to help,' said Tom. 'If you need anything give me a call.'

Andrew patted Tom on the shoulder. 'Thanks, lad. Enjoy the rest of your evening, both.'

Ellie watched him make his way over to Gran and saw how Gran's face lit up with joy when she saw him approach. Ellie turned away; she didn't want to be caught witnessing this private moment. She turned to Tom, who was grinning at her, his blue eyes alive with mischief. Her heart gave an unexpected wobble.

'Still finding your gran having a boyfriend a bit weird?' Tom asked.

'A bit,' she admitted.

'I think you're allowed. No one wants to see a beloved relative replaced,' he said seriously.

Ellie nodded, grateful that he understood.

'I do want her to be happy, though.'

Tom nodded and leaned on the table. Ellie was momentarily distracted by the muscles bunching under his T-shirt. She hurriedly returned her gaze to his face, hoping he hadn't noticed.

'I know you do. How's the investigation going?' he asked.

'A whiteboard was delivered today. It's got its own stand, which gives you an idea of the size of the thing. Gran had me set it up before we came out this evening. We've got Andrew's picture on the left side and Simon Hawley on the other. We were about to open a pack of coloured pens to start making bullet points of what we know but we ran out of time.'

Tom laughed. 'Laura's really getting into this crime-solving malarkey then?'

'Did you think she'd let it go?'

'I guess not.' Tom smiled. 'Is it causing you a lot of extra work?'

'Anything that takes her mind off the pain and her reduced mobility is a good thing. I did think I'd have more time to write my thesis over the summer but . . . '

'How's that going?'

'I've written two pages but I'm not happy with one of them.' Ellie pulled a face.

'Oh dear,' said Tom picking up his pint and draining the rest in one go. 'Would you and Laura like a lift home? I've only had the one.'

'I would love a lift home. I've been dreading getting Gran up that hill all evening. The only thing is, I'm not sure she's ready to leave yet,' said Ellie, flicking a glance at her grandmother who appeared to be still deep in conversation.

'I can wait,' said Tom, 'but I'd check with her. She's been getting tired easily after the fall. She probably has had enough.'

Ellie felt guilty for not thinking about that before and she rushed over to check.

'I would like to go home, yes, love,' said Gran, 'and how good of Tom to offer to drive us. We can show him our new whiteboard.'

Ellie laughed. 'Of course — why wouldn't he want to see that?'

'Don't be cheeky, Ellie,' said Gran with mock indignation. 'I'm sure he'll be interested — and there's something I wanted to discuss with you both. It's a new clue.'

Ellie was intrigued. What could Gran have found out this evening while sitting in the pub, and did it have anything to do with the significant look she'd given Ellie earlier?

* * *

Soon the three of them were in the dining room with Gran showing off her new purchase. The whiteboard took up the end wall of the room. It seemed a

102

little excessive considering they only had two of Gran's pencil drawings on it but when Ellie had pointed that out, Gran had insisted that the investigation would grow and they'd be grateful for the extra room.

'The whiteboard allows us to make easy-to-read notes,' Gran told Tom as she handed Ellie a pen. 'Ellie, you can write under each person their means, motivation and opportunity.'

'You've been watching too much American TV, Gran. That's not how things are done in the UK.'

'Does it matter?'

'I guess not,' conceded Ellie, amused.

She took the pen and started to make notes.

'We'll assume the motivation for each person is the money they would stand to gain,' Ellie stated as she made a note of that under each name. 'Andrew would get the insurance money and money from the sale of the meat, which we can assume is a substantial sum. Simon gets straight profit for the sale of the meat without the cost of keeping and rearing cattle.'

'There's not really any other reason for anyone to go to such trouble, other than for money,' Tom agreed.

'What does means actually stand for?' asked Gran sheepishly.

'Means is the ability to commit the crime,' explained Ellie. 'Andrew, for example, would have easy access to the cattle as he owns them and they were on his farm. We can say, therefore, that he has the means to commit the crime. Simon has stolen cattle before so we can assume he has access to cattle transporters and a place to dispose of livestock after he's stolen it. We can say, therefore, that he also has the means to commit the crime. Does that make sense?'

Gran nodded sagely. Tom grinned and winked at Ellie. She smiled back. The amateur investigation was more fun when Tom was around.

'Again, the opportunity to commit the crime is easier for Andrew because he's already on the site and we only have his word that the cows were taken at night. They could have been taken at any time of the day. We can say that he has plenty of opportunity. Without knowing whether Simon has an alibi for the night in question, we can assume he also has the opportunity. If I had access to the police's resources, establishing Simon's whereabouts that evening is where I would start.'

Ellie stood back and took a look at her notes.

'We've not really gained anything from this summation,' she said, 'other than to establish that they both could have done it.'

'If you're considering Andrew, then don't you also need to consider Roger as a suspect?' Tom asked.

Ellie duly put a line from Andrew and grudgingly wrote *Roger.* She'd liked him and Mary and didn't want them to be guilty — but Tom was right, if Andrew was a suspect then so were they.

'I've another suspect,' announced Gran.

Ellie sat down. Tom copied her and they waited for the big reveal. Ellie suspected Gran had been waiting hours for this moment.

'Charlotte's engaged,' she said, 'and you should see the size of the diamond on her engagement ring. It must have cost a fortune — and we all know there's no way Peter could afford that on his income.'

'Who's Peter?' asked Ellie.

'Charlotte's childhood sweetheart and now fiancé,' said Gran.

'He's also an odd-job man. I use him as a casual farmhand several times a year,' said Tom. 'He's done a bit of work for all of us farmers round here so he'd know how to handle different types of livestock. He's a good, reliable worker but you're right, it would be difficult for him to afford an expensive ring on what he earns.'

'It might not be a real diamond,' argued Ellie, not keen to be the person who could potentially destroy the lovely Charlotte's happiness. It was far better to blame the thefts on a stranger who was also a known criminal.

'I studied the ring more than you,' said Gran authoritatively. 'I'm confident it's real. What's more, she was boasting about her plans for her wedding and they're very lavish. It's going to cost a fortune.'

'She hasn't booked anything yet, has she?' protested Ellie. 'Every girl dreams of having a fairytale wedding — well, I don't, but a lot of women do. In reality it might be that all Peter and Charlotte can afford is a registry office wedding and a reception in the function room at The Ship. If she books Claridges for the reception then we should be suspicious.'

'Put Peter down on the board, Ellie,' said Gran.

It was only fair, as Ellie had ignored Gran's protests of Andrew's innocence. She put Peter's and Charlotte's names in the bottom right hand corner. Then in the bottom left-hand corner she put a big question mark.

'What's that for?' asked Gran.

'The question mark is to denote that the suspect could be someone completely random whom we don't know and may never consider,' said Ellie.

'How about proving that the people we have got on the list aren't guilty?' suggested Tom.

'Yes, Tom. That's a fabulous idea,' said Gran, sitting bolt upright, 'and it's a point I was just coming to.' She pulled out her pad and started searching through her notes.

'I was jotting down ideas earlier, and I think our strongest suspect is Simon Hawley.'

'The police will be investigating him,' Ellie said.

'We don't know that for sure,' said Gran. 'Also, time is of the essence. If he got rid of those cows and the sheep, then he has to have done it very recently. The trail may no longer be hot but it's probably quite warm.'

Ellie nodded. 'So what do you think we should do next?'

Gran sat back in her chair, momentarily unsure.

'We could go to Boxcomb and see if we can find anything about Simon's recent movements,' suggested Tom.

'Yes! That's a brilliant idea, Tom,' said Gran, snapping upright again.

'How far away is Boxcomb?' asked Ellie.

'About two hours by car,' said Tom.

'I don't want to put a dampener on things, but you would find sitting in a car for twenty minutes uncomfortable. How are we going to get you to Boxcomb?' Ellie asked her gran gently.

Gran sighed and sank back down. Tom dug into his coat pocket and pulled out his keys.

'I'd best be going,' he said. 'It's getting late.'

'I'll see you out,' said Ellie.

'Wait!' said Gran. 'I've an idea and — it's a bit of an imposition but I'll pay for the whole thing.'

'For what whole thing?' asked Ellie.

'You and Tom could go to Boxcomb. You could stay at the Farmers' Arms, it's a lovely pub. I stayed there with Grandad and I've always wanted to go back. Like I said, I'll pay.'

'Gran, I don't think we can ask Tom to take so much time away from his farm,' protested Ellie.

She did not want to spend a weekend alone with the tempting Tom. Not that he knew it, but he had the potential to derail all her carefully laid out plans. Already she was finding it hard to concentrate on anything but the size of his arms when he was standing next to her. She couldn't stop thinking what it would feel like to have them around her. She thought quickly.

'I could go on my own — but if I did, who's going to look after you?'

'I could stay with Andrew for the weekend and we could ask your parents to look after your farm — couldn't we, Tom?' said Gran, looking at Tom with large, hopeful eyes.

'Umm . . . ' said Tom.

'Gran, it's too much to ask him. I'm happy to go on my own,' insisted Ellie, the idea of an all-expenses weekend away quickly gaining appeal. Maybe she could use the opportunity to shop around for some new boots — she'd had no time for shopping since she'd arrived in Morwenna Bay.

'No, Ellie, it's fine. I'm sure Mum and Dad would be happy to look after the farm if they thought we were out and about solving crime.' He glanced at Ellie and winked.

Gran clapped her hands together.

'Oh, thank you both. It means the world to me that you'll do this. I'll make it up to you both, I promise.'

'Don't worry, Mrs Potts,' said Tom. 'An all-expenses trip to Boxcomb is payment enough. I'll look forward to it. Ellie, don't bother to see me out. I know the way. Goodnight, both.'

He grinned at Ellie and left.

Ellie stood watching him go and wondering how it was that she'd just agreed to go away with a man she barely knew. A man whom she was starting to find dangerously attractive.

7

Ellie pulled a hardback from the shelf, disturbing weeks of dust, which made her sneeze. She read the dust jacket, shook her head and returned the book to its place.

Standing in a library normally relaxed her, the rows of books comforting in their stillness. She'd been in this one for over half an hour and had yet to choose a single book — and the books weren't having their normal comforting effect either.

She couldn't concentrate. All she could think about was this trip to Boxcomb with Tom.

After Tom had left last night Ellie had tried to get Gran to tell Tom it wasn't necessary for him to go with her after all.

'He's a stranger, Gran. I'd feel uncomfortable going away with someone I barely know,' she'd protested.

Surely Gran should be more concerned about sending her only granddaughter away with a man. Wasn't she even slightly worried that Ellie might get ravished?

It seemed the thought had not crossed Gran's mind. Or, even more alarmingly, maybe it had and Gran wasn't worried about the thought.

'He's not a stranger. You've known him since you were both babies. You used to toddle around this very dining room together,' Gran had argued. 'I think of him as the grandson I never had. He'll be helpful because he knows the area and all about farming. He'll make a good sidekick.'

'We aren't Holmes and Watson,' Ellie had protested.

'I know. Ellie and Tom has a much nicer ring to it. Darling, you mustn't worry. Tom's said he's happy to go and I'm much happier knowing you'll have company. Now if you don't mind, love, I'd like to get ready for bed. I'm tired and I need to sleep off all that prosecco.'

Ellie had helped Gran with her night-time routine and then made her way to her own room and climbed into her large double bed. She'd picked up her novel and tried to read for a bit but she found she couldn't settle on the words. Every time she got to the end of a page, she realised she hadn't taken anything in. All she'd thought about was the weekend in Boxcomb.

It wasn't that she minded going off for a couple of days. It would be relaxing to have a rest from being a full-time carer, which was proving to be far more tiring than she'd anticipated. Gran wanted to go out most days, and getting anywhere was exhausting with all the preparation Ellie needed to do before they even set foot outside the door.

It also amazed her how badly most places were equipped to deal with wheelchairs. The sheer effort of getting Gran around was physically draining, but if they stayed in the house for a full day they would both develop severe cabin fever by the afternoon.

It wasn't the investigation that was bothering her either. She wouldn't mind a couple of days to find some evidence against this Simon Hawley character. She had a brief fantasy of triumphantly discovering the missing animals and restoring them to Andrew and Roger, but she dismissed it quickly. The chances of the livestock still being alive were very slim.

The problem with the weekend away was that she kept noticing how muscular Tom was and his smile had started doing something weird to her insides. She didn't need the distraction of him at this stage in her career. A weekend away with him could be dangerous.

* * *

Ellie tossed and turned all night and woke very unsettled early the next morning. She was glad when Jude came to visit Gran, meaning she could pop down into the village while they chatted. She needed the walk and the time alone to calm down.

She'd borrowed Gran's library card and was trying to find something to take her mind off all the things bothering her.

She pulled out another book but after reading the blurb it didn't appeal either, even though it was by one of her favourite authors. She put it back on the shelf and decided to give up. She'd treat herself to a coffee and a cake instead in The Cake Shop by the Sea, a café she'd spotted along the sea front. If cake couldn't restore her spirits nothing could.

The Café was tiny, obviously converted from someone's front room. It was decorated in pale blues and cream and was covered in photographs of the sea. Ellie loved it on sight. Its outdoor tables were full as people took advantage of the weather and sat eating cake while gazing across the bay. The inside was only slightly quieter, with a couple of tables free.

It was a difficult choice at the cake counter. The display was full of delicious treats and Ellie agonised for a few minutes over soft-looking chocolate brownies and muffins stuffed full of berries. In the end she settled for a tall Victoria sponge with a buttercream and jam filling and a long, cool drink of elderflower pressé.

By the time she'd finished choosing there was only one table left. It was crammed between a large pot plant and a low bookshelf but it was large enough for Ellie, and by the window.

From her vantage point she could see a row of brightly coloured houses and The Ship's beer garden, all facing the small Morwenna Bay. The tide was in and the sun sparkled across the gently undulating water.

Ellie couldn't manage to push Gran's chair across the soft sand, and so she hadn't visited the bay during this visit. Maybe she'd pop down while Gran was engrossed in *EastEnders* later. She wanted to feel the sand under her feet.

She sighed; she probably wouldn't have time later. Once Gran was settled in front of the TV Ellie had to clear up or prepare for the next day and if there was any time, she really needed to work on her thesis. She'd made very slow progress so far. She'd written nearly an entire chapter but she wasn't happy with the work. The words felt stilted and they didn't really convey the passion she felt for the subject.

She looked longingly at the beach again. Next year she'd come and visit Gran for a holiday and she'd spend as much time on the beach as she could. She took a big forkful of the springy sponge and tasted the sweetness on her tongue.

'Do you mind if I join you?' asked a soft voice. She looked up to see Charlotte smiling shyly.

'Of course not,' Ellie said. 'I'd love a bit of company.'

'Great,' said Charlotte, putting her

own piece of cake on the table. 'It's really wonderful to meet you finally. Your gran talks about you all the time so I feel I've known you for a really long time.'

Ellie felt her heart squeeze with love as she thought about Gran. She was lucky to be loved so wholeheartedly. She wasn't sure she deserved it.

'How are the plans for the wedding going?' she asked, changing the subject.

'Really well, thanks,' gushed Charlotte. 'We've already booked St Mary's, the village church, for the wedding ceremony. Peter and I have been going there since we were children so it's going to be special to be married by the same man who christened us both. I haven't decided on the reception yet because I'm not sure where we can hire somewhere large enough for everyone we're inviting. I thought about The Westerly on the outskirts of Boxcomb but I think they can only accommodate a hundred and fifty guests and I'm hoping for more than that.'

Ellie would have to ask Gran if The Westerly was an expensive place. A hundred and fifty plus seemed like a lot of guests and possibly quite pricey. But then what did she know? She'd never had to organise a wedding; maybe one hundred and fifty guests was normal.

Ellie wasn't sure she even knew that many people; she certainly didn't have that many friends and her family consisted of herself, her parents and Gran. If she ever married, she'd probably only be able to muster about ten guests. How depressing! She renewed her resolve to spend more time with her friends when she returned to London.

'Have you and Peter been together long?' she asked her companion.

'We've been together since our teens,' giggled Charlotte. 'But I knew he was the one for me when I was ten. I fell over in the playground and he carried me to the school nurse while I cried down his jumper. He was my hero then and he still is.' She glanced out of the window. 'He should be coming along the road about now. He's cutting Mr Jones' hedge this morning.'

Charlotte pointed to a garden in front of one of the brightly coloured houses. Its privet hedge was encroaching over the pathway and was in desperate need of a good hacking back.

'There he is,' said Charlotte excitedly. 'Isn't he handsome?'

Ellie had to agree that the young man approaching the hedge was rather good to look at. He had a hedge trimmer slung casually over one shoulder as if it weighed nothing and with his T-shirt off, Ellie could see a lot of his tall, muscular frame. His face and chest were a deep golden brown. His light brown hair was cut short and when he looked up and saw Charlotte waving to him from the café window, his smile was devastating. They would have stunning children.

'Wow,' said Ellie involuntarily.

'I know,' said Charlotte. 'I'm so lucky.' She turned and settled in her seat. 'He's not just broad shoulders and model good looks — he has the sweetest personality too,' she said as she cut out a mouthful of brownie. 'He's so caring and gentle, not to mention funny.'

Ellie felt a pang. She didn't need a boyfriend. She had her dream job, and every boyfriend she'd had so far had been a massive disappointment. But she couldn't deny that it would be good to have someone in her life who made her feel lucky to know them.

'Is the brownie good?' she asked weakly.

'It's fantastic. Have you met the owner of this café? I think she's called Catherine. She's new to the area and bakes all her own things. Here, you must try some.' Charlotte cut off a small piece of her brownie and deposited it on Ellie's plate.

Seeing as the morsel was already on her plate it would be rude not to eat it, so Ellie popped it in her mouth. The brownie more than lived up to expectations. The gooey chocolate simply melted on her tongue; she closed her eyes to savour it. She was definitely coming to The Cake Shop by the Sea again before she went back to London. She was going to work her way through every cake on the menu. It would be her place to escape to when looking after Gran and working on her thesis got too overwhelming.

'How about you?' asked Charlotte, taking Ellie by surprise. In the heaven of eating the brownie, she'd forgotten she wasn't alone.

'What do you mean?' she asked, confused.

'Is there a man waiting for you back in London or are you and Tom an item?'

Ellie choked on a mouthful of Victoria sponge.

'No to both!' she said. 'I've only met Tom a handful of times. I mean, I met him when we were younger but I don't remember much about him from that time. No, we aren't together. Why do you ask?'

'Oh, well, your gran is always talking about how Tom and her beautiful granddaughter would make a lovely couple,' said Charlotte guilelessly. 'It's her greatest wish.'

'Is it now?' said Ellie, shocked at the revelation.

Charlotte chatted on, only needing the barest of indications that Ellie was listening to carry on.

Ellie scooped up a few forkfuls of Victoria sponge and chewed them thoughtfully. Was Gran's desire to see Tom and Ellie hooked up the reason behind her insistence that Tom come with her to Boxcomb? Yes, Gran wanted the crime solved, but what if the visit to Boxcomb was less about tracking down this Simon Hawley guy than it was about throwing Tom and Ellie together?

No wonder she wasn't worried about Ellie getting ravished; she was probably hoping that's what would happen! She wouldn't put it past Gran who was very keen for Ellie to settle down.

Ellie felt very hot. What if Gran had only booked one room at the Farmer's Arms? What if Tom thought Ellie was actively involved in this matchmaking attempt? Was he embarrassed on her behalf at Gran's attempts to match-make her single granddaughter?

It wasn't as if he needed help getting a girlfriend. Ellie had noticed girls' heads turning the last two times they'd been in The Ship. It was she who needed help. She hadn't had a boy-friend in at least a year.

One thing was for certain — she was going to make sure she went to Boxcomb alone.

8

The sun streamed through the window, heating the pale blue duvet cover and releasing a strong smell of freshly laundered sheets. Ellie made her way over to the window and pushed the top pane of glass open.

A soft breeze flowed around her as Ellie stopped to take in the view. Just below her bedroom window, a river flowed gently over a rocky bed. A large weeping willow hung over the water and a family of five, their youngest member just able to take a few tottering steps, was picnicking under it. The other children giggled as the toddler plopped to her bottom and the mum leaned over to help her to her feet. She watched them for a moment, wishing she felt as carefree as they looked.

When she'd returned to Gran's house after meeting Charlotte in the café, Ellie had immediately taken Gran to task over her matchmaking attempts. Gran had insisted that setting up Tom and Ellie was the last thing on her mind.

'I used to think the two of you would be perfect together but now I see that you would never suit,' she declared as Ellie had banged around the kitchen preparing lunch.

'Why's that?' Ellie had asked, mildly offended even though she was against the idea herself.

'He's content with his life here in the country and you've grown into a city girl,' Gran stated.

'I've only ever lived in cities. I've always been a city girl,' Ellie had protested.

'Ah, but when you were younger, nothing made you happier than coming to visit Grandad and me out here in the wilds of Wales. You were practically feral, climbing over the cliffs on the beach and befriending all the local animals. I used to think you would come and settle near us, but it wasn't meant to be.'

'But . . . ' Ellie had said.

'Don't worry, sweetheart. I'm not upset. You know how proud I am of you and your fabulous career. I wouldn't want it any other way. You've been so kind to come and look after me and I know this investigation is making life even busier, but it's so important to me. I haven't told you yet but the insurance company are being difficult with Andrew. If he doesn't get his farm back on track then it will ruin him. I don't mean financially, I mean it's his life. Without his farm he won't be the man I know and have grown to love.'

After this heartfelt speech, Ellie had hugged Gran tightly and then gone to pack her bags. She could survive a weekend with Tom; she'd just avoid looking at his gorgeous shoulders.

She turned away from the window and opened her suitcase. It had only been a two-hour drive to Boxcomb but the day was warm and she'd become hot and sticky in the car. She needed a shower to freshen up, and a change of clothes. She pulled out of her overnight bag a lemon summer dress with spaghetti straps and a scooped neckline. Bold flowers ran along its edging; it was one of her favourite outfits. It wasn't the most practical of clothing for an afternoon of investigating, but was definitely the most refreshing item she owned.

The en-suite was newly refurbished with a sleek walk-in shower and a large rain head. Once she'd worked out how to switch it on Ellie stood under the powerful jet for five minutes allowing the coolness of the water to soak into her bones. She thought about her shower at home. It barely dribbled out water. She needed to get it replaced with one of these, although she'd probably never leave the flat if she did. It was so luxurious she felt relaxed and refreshed after a few minutes.

She towel-dried her long hair and

then tied it into a messy bun, clipping a few stray wisps with some grips. The wide neck of her summer dress allowed her to step into it and when she'd slipped her arms through the straps, she checked the mirror. She looked much better than the hot, sweaty mess that had arrived half an hour ago. She debated whether to put on make-up but decided against it. She didn't want Tom to think she was making an effort on his behalf.

Ellie picked up her handbag, checked she had her phone and her room key and stepped out into the narrow corridor outside her room. She'd agreed to meet Tom downstairs so that they could find somewhere to eat lunch before heading off to look for clues.

⋆   ⋆   ⋆

Tom was waiting for her at a table on the pub's terrace. The seats overlooked the river she had seen from her bedroom window and the gentle burble of the water drowned out the conversation of the other diners.

'Hi,' he said. 'You look lovely.' However he was frowning as he watched her approach.

'What's wrong?' she asked as she pulled out a wooden chair and sat down, a welcoming breeze lifting the ends of her dress and cooling her legs.

'You know the places we might be visiting will probably be grubby,' he said. 'You could ruin that pretty dress.'

'It's too hot for me to wear jeans. If there's any dirty work needed this afternoon, you can do it,' she said, gesturing to his worn jeans and faded blue, cotton T-shirt.

Tom laughed. 'Fair enough. I thought we should eat lunch here. The food's meant to be good and I checked behind the bar — Laura's put a decent kitty together for us for food. All we have to do is give our room numbers and we should be able to eat here for most of our meals. Also, I've been thinking. After lunch there are a couple of places we could go and take a look at.'

'Where's that?' asked Ellie, picking up a menu.

'Let's order and then I'll tell you.'

Ellie chose a goat's cheese salad with pine nuts and pomegranate seeds and a tall glass of ice-cold lime and soda.

Tom went up to the bar to order and Ellie looked out onto the river again. The picnicking family had moved on and ducks were waddling around the area looking for scraps of food.

Tom returned with the drinks and Ellie downed half of hers before asking Tom again, 'So where do you think we should go this afternoon?'

'I think we should try and find out what Simon's been up to since he got out of jail and whether he's in regular contact with the rest of the gang also responsible for stealing cattle the last time he was in business. I've got a short list of names for us to go through.'

'Without access to the local police database, how are we going to find these people?'

'I just asked at the bar.'

'What!' Ellie gasped, whipping her head round to glance at the barman. 'That's hardly stealthy sleuthing, is it?'

Tom laughed, 'I've known the landlord for a long time. He's from Morwenna Bay originally. He's not a fan of Simon and his lot. They've been troublemakers for years and the locals have had enough. He said he'd write down a list of where he thinks they all are now.'

Ellie nodded and took another refreshing sip of her drink. It wasn't a good idea for people to know what they were doing in Boxcomb. She didn't want the word to get back to Simon and his gang. Unnecessarily annoying known criminals was a bad idea — but Tom had already asked so she just had to hope that the barman was discreet.

'Where else do you have in mind?' she asked.

'If we agree that someone opportunistically took Roger's sheep, then the chances are quite high that the thief

would need to store the sheep somewhere before moving them on. I've
been thinking about this a lot since I
first found out that Andrew's cows were
taken. You can't just dump a whole load
of cows or sheep in a back garden shed.
You'd need a large space. Just outside
town is a port with several warehouses
suitable for keeping livestock. It's
probably the easiest place to store them
locally and it's the most strategic
because it's on the way to the M4 and
two of the Welsh abattoirs. It should be
a fairly easy place to check out and
cross off our list if I'm way off the
mark.'

Ellie nodded in agreement.

'OK, it's worth a shot. Let's go there
first. If we find out that someone's been
using a warehouse for storage we may
be able to find out fairly easily who's
renting the building. Is The Westerly
anywhere near the dock? If so, could we
swing by and take a look at it on our
way.'

'It's a short detour but it will only

add ten minutes to our journey to go and see it. Why are you interested?'

'Charlotte wants to have her reception there,' Ellie told him.

Tom whistled. 'The Westerly is very swanky. I'd imagine it would cost a bit for a reception there.'

Ellie's heart sank.

'Does Charlotte have a good job?' she asked. 'By that I mean, is she paid well?'

'She works part-time at the Post Office,' Tom said, pulling a face.

'Are either of their parents wealthy?' asked Ellie clutching at straws.

Tom shook his head sadly, 'I'm afraid I don't know where Peter and Charlotte's new wealth is coming from.'

'OK,' said Ellie decisively. 'Let's go and see The Westerly and then head to the dock.'

'Sounds like a plan,' said Tom as their food arrived.

Ellie tucked in, grateful that her salad had come with a side of warm, crunchy ciabatta bread. She'd not thought to order any but now that she took a bite, she realised she was so hungry that a salad on its own would not have been enough — especially as Tom had ordered himself a thick cheeseburger and curly fries.

They ate in silence for a while. Tom eventually broke the silence by telling Ellie about how Tilly had walked straight into a pond covered in algae during a walk yesterday and had been so shocked to find herself covered in water that she'd just stood there for a few seconds until she'd leaped out and covered Tom in green slime. Ellie fell a little more in love with the adorable Border collie.

'Should we get pudding?' Tom asked as they finished their meal.

'As Gran's paying I shall say yes,' said Ellie. 'In fact, I already know what I want.'

'Is it the strawberries with lemon sorbet and the Pimm's topping?'

'How did you know?'

'By using my excellent deduction

skills,' Tom said, grinning. 'Plus that's what I'm having. It looks like the best thing on the menu.'

'If you apply those skills this afternoon, we'll have this case solved in no time. I'll go and order this time. Would you like another drink?'

'Yes, thanks. I'll have another cola, please.'

Ellie went up to the bar and took her time ordering. She was enjoying this relaxing lunch and didn't want it to end. The thought of traipsing around the town looking for some men who may or may not be guilty didn't appeal to her. She had enough of that in her actual job.

She picked up the drinks and looked at Tom. She'd far rather spend her afternoon sitting by the river with this funny, handsome man . . .

Shocked, she put her drink back on the bar. She was supposed to be ignoring the fact that Tom was handsome, not adding to his attractiveness by finding him funny. She was going to have to toughen up.

She glanced at Tom from her position at the bar. He was sitting facing the river, his long legs stretched out in front of him. His arms were relaxed, one resting on the table and the other on his lap. As if he sensed her watching him he turned and smiled at her and her stomach did a strange flip flop. Yes, he was a handsome man — but that didn't mean she was attracted to him. The weird wobbly feeling was down to embarrassment at being caught staring.

She picked up the drinks and walked back.

'The desserts will be five minutes,' she said.

'Great,' he answered.

For the rest of the meal they discussed their plan of attack. Ellie made a point of keeping all talk strictly about the case just in case he'd taken the sight of her gazing at him the wrong way.

By the time they'd finished their refreshing dessert she was more than ready to get going.

'Are you missing Tilly?' Ellie asked as they climbed into the Volvo.

'A bit,' he said with a smile, 'but I doubt she's missing me. She has a bottomless pit of love and happiness and seems to find joy whoever she's with. She'll be having a better weekend with my parents at the farm than sitting in the hot car.'

He drove for five minutes before they came to The Westerly. Even the sign was grand; edged in gold foil, it was discreet and classy. They travelled down a short driveway bordered by manicured lawns. The hotel was a large, red-brick manor house with sweeping steps leading up to a grand entrance. It did not look cheap.

'Do you want to go in?' asked Tom.

Ellie let out a long breath. Did she need to see inside? It was clearly an expensive hotel.

'It looks luxurious,' she commented.

'Yeah, it is. I've been to a wedding there before and it's something else. I was going to stay the night but I would

140

have blown half my annual holiday budget on a room, so I drove instead.'

'I don't need to go in,' said Ellie. 'I've seen enough to know you have to have money to be considering this as your wedding venue.'

Tom nodded thoughtfully. 'If anything, I'd say it was too much money.'

'What do you mean?' asked Ellie, confused.

'There have only been two thefts. If Peter's behind them, then I'm not convinced he'd have made enough money to pay for this place. I mean, think about it. Yes, whoever stole the cattle would have made a hefty profit but there would have been some outlay too. There's the hire or purchase of a transporter and somewhere to store the livestock. I don't think the raids can have been done by one person either — so the profits would have to split at least two ways.'

'Agreed, but Peter's share of the profits could be supplementing the savings he and Charlotte already have,'

Ellie pointed out reluctantly.

'Hmmm,' said Tom. It appeared he wasn't keen on Peter being their suspect either.

He turned the car without further comment.

★ ★ ★

Boxcomb's port wasn't what Ellie was expecting. It was small and run-down. It obviously wasn't used much any more and the attached warehouses were rusty and grubby.

'How do you want to do this?' Ellie asked as Tom slowed to look for a parking space.

'You know more about this sort of thing than me. I'll follow your lead.'

She nodded, glad that he didn't automatically want to take charge. Tom found a turning for the warehouses' car park and he pulled into the only space in the tiny car park.

'I think we'll play it straight and tell whoever's in the reception that we're investigating some thefts. It's always best to stick to the truth.'

They made their way to a large blue Portakabin with a sign announcing that this was the port's reception. Ellie pushed open a rusty, heavy door and found a teenager sitting behind a large desk flicking through an old, crumpled magazine.

The girl leaped up with the delight of a terminally bored person finding something to do.

'Hello,' she said brightly, 'how can I help you?'

Ellie smiled. Hopefully this would be easy.

'Hi. I'm Ellie Potts and this is my partner, Thomas Owens. We're investigating a crime on behalf of two farmers from Morwenna Bay. We're looking for some information about some stolen livestock and we were wondering if you would be able to help us with our inquiry.'

The young woman's eyes widened in alarm and Ellie hid a smile.

'I don't know anything about stolen livestock,' the girl said, her voice rising in pitch.

'Don't worry,' said Ellie, smiling gently, 'we're not accusing you of anything. We're just trying to establish whether someone could have used one of the warehouses to house animals in the last few weeks. If so, there's a possibility that it could be related to a case we're investigating.'

The girl nodded, visibly relaxing.

'I only help out here now and then. I'm normally at college. But we've definitely had some animals through recently.'

Ellie's heart pounded. Could it be this easy?

'Could you help us out with any further details?' she asked.

'The paperwork will be in here somewhere,' said the girl, gesturing to the filing cabinets behind her. 'But I'm not sure where. Dad's doing the night shift later. He starts at eight tonight so you could come back then. I'm sure he'd be happy to help.'

'What's your father's name?' asked Ellie.

'David Banks, and I'm Sookie Banks.'

'Thank you, Sookie. You've been a great help. If you could let your dad know that we'll be calling back later, we'd appreciate it. In the meantime do you remember what animals came through recently?'

'The most recent animals I'm aware of were sheep,' Sookie said without hesitation.

'When do you think they were here?' asked Ellie her heart starting to race.

'This coming Wednesday, it will have been three weeks ago. I'm sure about that because that was the last time I was here. I remember them really well, because we don't get many animals and these ones looked weird.'

'In what way?' asked Ellie.

'They were mostly white but they all had a large black stripe running down the underside of their bodies.' Sookie waved her hand under her neck and down to her stomach to illustrate.

And just like that, it seemed they'd found what had happened to Roger's sheep.

9

Tom sat on the edge of the bed and pulled a clean T-shirt out of his rucksack. He'd just had time for a quick shower to wash away the stickiness of the afternoon before he and Ellie were going out again. He rubbed his hands over his eyes and resisted the temptation to lie back on the bed. He was so tired, but there was no time for the sleep he desperately wanted.

He'd been sleeping badly since the thefts of cattle had begun. Any slight noise at night and he was up and out of bed, checking no one had breached his thick padlock and chain.

Installing the CCTV hadn't relaxed him. It would only show him images of his animals being taken. It wouldn't help him get them back — and losing them would be a financial nightmare.

He'd thought he would be constantly on edge being so far away from the farm, but the opposite had happened. As he'd driven out of Morwenna Bay he'd felt his shoulders relaxing and his normal good humour resurfacing.

It could be because he was doing something proactive rather than waiting for a calamity to befall him and his farm. Or his refreshed mood could be because of the mammoth crush he was developing on Laura Potts' grand-daughter.

He sighed and shook his head. It was such an unbelievably bad idea to develop feelings for a woman who had made it clear so many times she was not interested in him, or in relationships in general. Even worse an idea was to spend uninterrupted time with her which might allow that crush to develop into something stronger. He should have listened to his head and not have come on this trip but the temptation of being with Ellie for two days without any other demands on her time had been too much.

He wanted to see if he could break through the barriers she'd erected around herself. Sometimes he thought he was getting through, but then they seemed to slam back up. He couldn't for the life of him think why. He didn't think she found him unattractive; she'd tried to hide it but he'd caught her gazing at him occasionally and he prided himself on being a good person, so what was the problem?

Laura had started to tell him something when they'd briefly been left alone. She'd seemed to suggest the problem lay with Ellie's childhood and her parents moving around a lot. Laura hadn't been able to finish telling him whatever it was before Ellie had frustratingly come back into the room.

Could Laura have been trying to tell him that Ellie needed stability? It wasn't as if a relationship with him would be unstable, so perhaps he'd misunderstood. It was more likely he'd misinterpreted her gaze and she wasn't interested in him in that way. He'd have to be brave and just come out and ask her out on a date. He'd asked girls out before; he could manage it again. If she said no he'd have his answer.

Decision made, he slipped the T-shirt over his head and straightened it out over his stomach. A quick glance at the clock showed him he was running a few minutes late. He pulled on his trainers and made sure he had everything he needed for the evening ahead.

He found Ellie waiting in the hotel's lobby. She'd changed into jeans and a T-shirt and he was grateful. He didn't think he'd be able to concentrate on what they were doing if he was confronted by her in that dress again.

'Sorry I'm a bit late,' he said.

'Don't worry, I only just got down here too. Shall we get going?'

'Sure. Let's hope David Banks is as accommodating as his daughter.'

They both climbed into the car. It was hot and stuffy and Tom turned on the engine quickly so they could wind down the windows.

After their success at the port, the rest of the afternoon had been unenlightening. They'd found where most of Simon Hawley's previous gang were working. They'd even caught sight of a few of them going about their jobs, but that hadn't produced any leads. They'd stopped for a quick bite in the pub restaurant before heading up to their rooms.

'When Gran suggested this investigation I imagined we'd be sitting in her comfortable home discussing the case in the same way we'd discuss a crossword,' she said ruefully. 'I never imagined I'd be in a different town from Gran, interviewing people I don't know. I feel like we should set up our own private investigation firm after this. We're acquiring all the necessary skills.'

Tom laughed. 'We could be the next Holmes and Watson.'

'So long as I get to be Holmes then I'm up for that,' Ellie responded.

This time the only space in the car

park was taken up by a large four-wheel drive. Tom drove down the road and found a space in an empty office car park not far away. It had just gone half past eight, so Sookie's father should have arrived and made himself comfortable by now.

David Banks looked nothing like his daughter. He was as wide as he was tall, with a bright red face and owl-like glasses perched on the end of a thick nose. His undersized suit stretched tightly across his lumpy shoulders.

'How can I help you?' he asked officiously, as they made their way into his office.

Ellie introduced them. 'We're working on behalf of farmers Andrew Parkin and Roger Weekes. Two weeks ago they were both victims of theft. Thieves broke into barns on their respective farms in Morwenna Bay and stole cows and sheep.

'Earlier your daughter described some sheep she said she'd seen being deposited into one of the warehouses here. The description sounds like a strong match to some of the missing livestock. We'd be very grateful if you could help us with any more information so that we can either eliminate these sheep from our enquiries or we can move forward with our investigation.'

David nodded. 'Ah yes, Sookie did mention your visit. I should be able to dig out some paperwork for the relevant warehouse. Please take a seat.'

Ellie and Tom sat as David rummaged around in an ancient, overflowing filing cabinet. It squealed on its runners as David pulled drawers towards him. Tom grimaced as he shifted in his seat and realised his trousers had stuck slightly to the surface. Ellie moved to put her bag on the floor and then seemed to think better of it. She rested it on her lap instead and pulled out her notebook.

'There's only been one company who have brought animals into the complex during the last few months,' said David as he pulled out a wodge of paper with a flourish. 'A company called Morwen Ltd rented out warehouse C for a period of six months. Our logs show that they have accessed the warehouse four times to date.'

'That is incredibly helpful information, Mr Banks. May I just check I've got the spelling of the company correct?' Ellie repeated the spelling back to him.

'That's correct,' said David.

'Did the company provide an address?'

'Yes.' David flicked through the papers. 'All our customers are required to provide an address and telephone number.'

He gave Ellie both and she wrote them down in her notebook.

'Would you like to see inside the warehouse?' asked David.

'If that's possible, then I think it would be helpful — thank you,' said Ellie.

'I doubt there's anything in there,' said David. 'We'd have heard if animals were being kept in there for long periods. If my recollection serves me right, the sheep were there for less than twenty-four hours. You're welcome to take a look, though.'

David opened the large, rusty safe that hung on the wall above the desk.

'This is the spare key for warehouse C. Please return it when you've finished. It's on the left, clearly labelled so you shouldn't have any problems — but if you do, don't hesitate to pop back and I'll see if I can help you.'

Ellie took the key and thanked him. They stepped out of the cramped room and Tom gulped lungfuls of fresh air. The Portakabin hadn't seemed so awful this afternoon; perhaps it was David who was responsible for its current sticky, claustrophobic feeling.

'Do you think we should call the police?' Tom asked as they walked down a central road lined with dilapidated buildings. The complex had seen better days.

'Let's take a look inside first and then

decide,' said Ellie. 'This could be a false lead.'

Tom shrugged and followed. Dusk was falling but the air didn't feel as fresh as it did on the farm, where he could often smell the sea breeze from his fields. Here, the air smelled dusty and stale. He couldn't imagine working in that sticky Portakabin every day. How depressing not to be able to feel the wind in your hair as you worked.

★ ★ ★

They found warehouse C easily. There was a large double door at the front but this was padlocked with a thick chain and a sturdy bolt. Tom spotted a smaller side door on the edge of the building. The key they'd been given fitted into its lock and the door swung open easily. They stepped inside; it was dark and empty. The air felt damp against Tom's skin and the sickly sweet smell of decaying manure was almost overwhelming.

'Can you see a light switch?' Ellie asked.

Tom felt the wall beside him, 'Here's something,' he said. He flicked a switch but the cavernous room remained in darkness.

Tom reached into his pocket and pulled out his mobile phone. 'I've got a torch on here,' he said. 'Hold on while I switch it on.'

After a few seconds scrolling through various apps he found what he was looking for and he flicked the light on. He turned the beam to the switch he'd pressed.

'This looks like it is a light switch,' he said, 'but it doesn't seem to work.'

He flipped it a couple of times just to make sure but the room remained in darkness.

'Your torch is bright. If we stick together we should be able to see well enough — although we can smell that animals have been kept in here without having to look.'

Tom shone the torch at the floor.

Sure enough heaps of dung covered the area in front of him and for as far as the narrow beam of light could reach. The floor was wet and he doubted the room was ventilated. It didn't look as if any bedding had been put out either. He hoped the animals hadn't been kept here for long, because these were terrible conditions.

He knew then that there was no way Andrew could be involved in any of this. He was a campaigner for animal welfare and it would break his heart to know that his animals had been kept in conditions like these. It was good to know for sure that his friend was innocent — not that he'd doubted him for a second.

'Did you hear that?' asked Ellie, her hand reaching out to grab his arm.

'Hear what?'

'It sounds like a car heading towards us.'

They stood in silence for a second and listened. Seconds later, the engine stopped close by. A door opened and slammed. Footsteps crunched in their direction.

Without thinking, Tom turned off his torchlight and roughly pulled Ellie behind some empty crates just as a key sounded in the padlock.

10

Ellie's heart was racing. This whole situation was crazy. Why were they in this warehouse? Why hadn't she phoned the local police like Tom had suggested?

Now she had endangered him by dragging him into a room with a potentially hostile person. Their cover would only work if the light switch by the door didn't work either. If it did then their hiding place would be revealed instantly. What possible reason could they give for hiding in an empty warehouse?

The warehouse door creaked open and a dark figure stood in silhouette at the entrance.

Tom slid his fingers into hers and she squeezed his hand tightly. She'd never forgive herself if something happened to him.

The figure stepped into the building

and appeared to be feeling the wall for the light switch.

Ellie held her breath. Beside her she felt Tom do the same.

They heard the click of the light switch and then a hiss of annoyance when nothing happened. The figure disappeared, and the sound of a van door being opened reached them in their hiding place.

Over the next few minutes Ellie and Tom watched as the figure hauled several large sacks into the warehouse. After five trips he seemed to be done and he stood still for a minute, hands on hips facing into the room. Then whoever it was turned and walked out, closing the door of the warehouse with a bang. The sounds of metal scraping against metal grated through the warehouse as if the padlock was being secured.

For a few moments there was silence. Then Ellie heard a van door shut and seconds later, an engine starting up and driving away.

Tom and Ellie stayed where they were for a few minutes longer. When all they could hear was bird song from the trees outside, they both stood up and Ellie let out a shaky breath.

'That was close,' she said in a voice that wasn't quite her own.

Tom nodded.

'Let's go,' he said keeping his fingers threaded through hers.

'Wait,' she said urgently. 'Let's see what's been left here.'

Tom turned his torch back on and they picked their way across the warehouse floor.

'They're sacks of animal feed,' said Tom dully as they got close enough for his light to pick up the writing on the outside of the bags.

Ellie pulled out her phone and took a few snaps of the food and the empty barn. She popped her phone back in her bag and nodded.

'OK — we don't need to see any more.'

They made their way back to

reception, Tom dragging Ellie behind him. At the Portakabin Tom let go of Ellie's hand and shoved open the door, which banged into the wall behind it. Ellie immediately missed the contact of his warm skin.

'Why did you let that man come through when you knew we were in there?' Tom shouted.

Ellie jumped back in surprise. She hadn't realised Tom was furious but now, as she looked at him, she could see that his fists were clenched and the skin on his neck was an angry red.

'What man?' asked David, clearly confused.

'The man who just drove down to warehouse C and came inside while we were searching it. The man who could very well have been armed and dangerous and who is definitely responsible for at least two serious crimes. *That* man,' Tom ground out.

'I'm sorry,' said David shamefacedly. 'I was watching the wrestling and I didn't see anyone go past.'

David held up his mobile which was playing a wrestling match. The figures looked tiny from where Ellie was standing.

Tom let out a huff of frustration and leaned against the cabin wall, rubbing his face.

'Ellie could have been hurt,' he said, his voice quieter.

'I'm really very sorry,' said David.

'There's no harm done,' said Ellie softly, stepping forward so that she was in line with Tom. 'We'll be calling the police with our findings so they'll probably be in touch with you in the next few days. We'd be very grateful if you could help them in any way possible.'

'Of course,' said David.

'Let's go now, Tom,' she said, tugging his T-shirt. Tom stepped away from the wall, looked at David and shook his head. He strode out of the office ahead of Ellie, who turned and shrugged apologetically at David before following Tom out.

★　★　★

He was almost back at the car before she caught up with him.

'I'm sorry about my outburst,' he said gruffly.

'That's OK,' said Ellie. 'Shock makes us all react differently.'

'I just keep thinking of what could have happened. What if he'd had some kind of weapon? I wouldn't have been able to defend you.'

'You're forgetting I'm a self-defence expert,' said Ellie lightly.

Tom huffed out a laugh. 'You're right — I'd forgotten that. It would have been you saving me, wouldn't it?'

'Of course. I could definitely have taken him.'

Tom smiled, but it didn't reach his eyes.

'Let's get back to the hotel,' said Ellie. 'We've got some more research to do, and after that we can decide our next move.'

They both got back in the car and

Tom started the engine. He was still frowning and every few seconds he shook his head crossly as he drove back to the Farmer's Arms. Ellie didn't like to see the tight lines around his eyes; she wanted happy, laughing Tom back.

'Why do they call you Tearaway Tom?' she asked to distract him from his dark mood.

Tom glanced at her in surprise. 'Why are you asking about that now?' he said.

'I've always wanted to know. I asked my mum when I was younger but she refused to talk about it. I figured it had to be something pretty bad, otherwise why not tell me?'

Tom sighed theatrically.

'I'm not about to tell you about my dodgy past, am I?' he said, a laugh creeping into his voice.

'I promise that if I end up using your stories in my research or teaching modules you will remain completely anonymous,' said Ellie grinning.

Tom pretended to be considering her offer.

166

'No,' he said eventually, 'if your mum didn't think you were old enough to hear about my indiscretions then I don't think I should tell you.'

'I should warn you, I've been trained in interrogation techniques,' Ellie teased.

It wasn't quite true. She'd had lectures on interrogation when she was a student — but that didn't sound quite as dramatic.

Tom laughed and the tension lines around his eyes smoothed. 'Do your worst,' he challenged.

'Did you steal something?'

'What? No! Of course I didn't steal something. Tearaway is another name for 'toe rag' not 'criminal mastermind'. You've got to remember Morwenna Bay is basically crime free so any misdemeanour is a big deal. My everything-I-own-must-be-black phase was the worst of it. I listened to loud music and grew my hair long — honestly, that's about it.'

'You folded pretty quickly there,' remarked Ellie, smiling.

Tom laughed. 'Yeah, you got me. I'm going to have to put my career as an international jewel thief on hold. I crack too easily under pressure.'

'So why the black phase? Were you a Goth?'

'No, I had a depressingly one-sided crush on a girl. I decided she would notice me if I was different. It was a stand-out-from-the-crowd thing.'

'Did it work?'

'No.'

'Would I know the girl? Was it Charlotte? I bet it was. She's so beautiful, I bet there isn't a man our age who hasn't been in love with her at least once in their life.'

'It wasn't Charlotte.'

'Who was it then?'

'We're back,' announced Tom unnecessarily as he pulled into the Farmer's Arms car park. 'Shall we get a drink and discuss our next move?'

'OK,' said Ellie unfastening her seat belt once Tom had switched off the engine. 'But don't think I've forgotten we're in the middle of a conversation here.'

'I think you'll find we've come to the end of that particular conversation.' He grinned across at her in the darkening car.

Ellie smiled back and thought it would be impossible to know Tom and not have a tiny crush on him. She was certainly struggling to keep herself level-headed around him and she was sworn off relationships of any kind.

The girl had probably noticed him well enough but hadn't been mature enough to act on it. She wasn't about to inflate his ego and tell him that.

★　★　★

Even though it was getting late, the evening air was still warm. They found a secluded area on the terrace after getting some drinks at the bar; a large glass of Sauvignon Blanc for Ellie and a pint of Carw Haf for Tom.

'First order of business,' said Ellie,

pulling her smart phone out of her handbag, 'is to see whether Morwen Ltd is a real company.'

She tapped the name into the search engine.

'Nothing comes up,' she said.

'What about the company address?'

'It does exist but it's a residential property in the middle of Boxcomb. We'll check it out tomorrow, but the chances are it's a dead end.'

'And the phone number?'

'It doesn't show up as being registered to a company. We'll call it tomorrow and see what happens. It doesn't look as if our friend David Banks takes his security measures at the warehouses very seriously. He's probably too busy watching TV on his phone.'

Tom took a sip of his pint and watched the meandering river for a moment.

'I'm sorry about my outburst earlier,' he said.

'Don't worry about it. It caused a

great distraction.'

'For what?'

Ellie held up the key to the warehouse.

'You stole the warehouse key!'

'I didn't steal it. I merely forgot to return it in the heat of the moment,' said Ellie, grinning.

'That's what they all say. I'll visit you when you're doing time at Her Majesty's pleasure.'

Ellie giggled and then sobered.

'It felt like a good thing to have. Those sacks of animal feed can mean only one thing,' she said.

'He's going to strike again,' Tom confirmed grimly.

11

'It's not Andrew,' said Tom as he turned the ignition in the car the following morning.

Ellie pushed her slightly damp hair away from her face. When it flopped back down again she pulled some grips out of her handbag and slid them through her hair. An early start had been her idea, but she wished she'd factored in time to style her hair properly. She felt bedraggled.

At the least the damp hair was cooling. It was only just after eight and already the air outside was warm; in the car it was stifling.

'Tell me why you think that,' she challenged.

'The man standing in the doorway yesterday evening wasn't Andrew.'

'And we're sure it was a man because . . . '

'Build, height and the way he moved. Plus that hiss he made was masculine.'

'So you don't think it's Andrew because . . . '

'The silhouette was all wrong. The person was much broader and stronger than Andrew. Andrew's like a bean-pole.'

'I agree,' said Ellie.

'Also, Andrew would never keep animals in conditions like that.'

Ellie nodded. From the little she knew of Andrew she had already guessed this to be the case.

'It wasn't Roger either,' said Tom confidently.

'Yeah, I agree,' said Ellie. 'From our limited suspect list that leaves us with Simon Hawley, Peter and Mr Question Mark.'

Tom nodded. 'Or a combination of all three,' he said as he took a left turn.

'These streets are very narrow,' Ellie observed as they made their way through a rabbit warren of terraced houses. They'd arrived early, hoping to catch the residents of the address Morwen Ltd. had provided as the company headquarters.

'They're also, annoyingly, mostly one-way,' said Tom. 'We passed the end of the road we want about five minutes ago but now we're going round in circles trying to get to the entrance.'

Tom took another turn and then another.

'This is it,' he said as they turned up yet another narrow road.

Smart terraced houses with brightly coloured front doors lined both sides of the road. This was a road that was proud of its heritage and which made an effort to keep the old houses looking bright and clean. It reminded Ellie of the street she lived on in London, although she couldn't afford a whole house. She was proud of her top floor flat; it was bought with her own money, but she wished she could afford to buy a house, especially one like this.

'There's number forty-two,' said Ellie as they passed a house not quite as smart as the rest.

Tom parked the car and they climbed out. Ellie straightened her dress. She'd chosen a pale blue one this morning with a V neckline and short sleeves. It wasn't as cool as her yellow dress from yesterday and already she could feel stickiness at the back of her neck.

'Nervous?' asked Tom.

'No. We'll stick to the cold-caller disguise. It's not as if we're performing an arrest or anything. We just want to know whether anyone in the house is connected to Morwen Ltd. If Simon Hawley's the owner then it's case closed, don't you think?'

Number forty-two had an air of desertion about it. Leaves had gathered by the front doorstep and it looked as if no footsteps had disturbed them for weeks. Tiny weeds were sprouting around the edges of the gravel front garden and a telephone directory was gently rotting on the path to the front door. The house was smart but neglected.

Ellie knocked the door. No one answered. She knocked again.

Tom tried to peer through the net curtain hanging in the large bay window.

'I can't detect any movement,' Tom said.

'Can I help you?' asked a sharp voice.

Both Tom and Ellie flinched and turned quickly. A smart woman, with short grey hair worn in a tight bob was regarding them suspiciously.

Ellie panicked slightly; this wasn't in the plan. Then she remembered her earlier mantra; when in doubt, stick to the truth.

'Hello. We're looking for the owners of this property,' she said.

'Why? Is something wrong?' demanded the lady suspiciously.

'We're investigating some thefts on behalf of family friends and this property has been linked to the crimes. We're trying to establish whether the owners are involved.'

'If they are recent crimes then I very

much doubt it. The family are in France. They've been living there for six months. She's got a temporary job out there and it was too good an opportunity for them to miss. I'm not sure when, or if, they're coming back. The way of life seems to suit them.'

'Do you know the name of the company she's working for?' Ellie asked softly, not wanting to antagonise the lady who was currently their only hope of moving forward with the investigation.

'Gemini Printing Solutions,' said the lady.

'Do you know if anyone has rented the property from them while they're away?' Tom asked.

'I live next door and I can confirm that no one has been living there in the meantime.'

'Could you confirm the names of the owners for me?' asked Ellie.

'Cameron and Emily McKenzie and their two children, Anna and Jake,' the neighbour stated.

'Thank you so much for your help,' said Ellie. 'It sounds as if the owners aren't related to the crimes at all. Would you be able to contact them to let them know their address is being used fraudulently?'

The lady nodded and Ellie gave her a brief overview of the case.

'Another dead end,' said Tom as they traipsed back to the Volvo.

'The address was a long shot anyway.'

They climbed back into the car and sat in silence for a moment.

'I'll try the phone number again,' Ellie said.

She'd tried the number earlier this morning but it had gone straight through to answerphone. She had the same lack of success this time around.

'I'll keep trying but I think we can assume it's a defunct number,' she remarked.

Tom nodded and slid the key into the ignition.

'Shall we go and get some breakfast?' he asked.

'Definitely,' responded Ellie, suddenly feeling very tired and hungry. It was a long time since the meal they'd had evening before.

★ ★ ★

They headed into Boxcomb's quaint town centre and picked a café overlooking the central square with white metal seats outside the front window. Ellie scraped back a chair and sighed with relief as she sat down; the seats were much comfier than they looked. Even though the day hadn't been particularly active yet, she'd felt tired with disappointment.

She'd not really expected anything from the house or the telephone number but she'd hoped they would lead to another clue. As it was they were essentially, if not quite back to the beginning, still pretty near it. She picked up a menu and started reading through it. Tom did the same.

'The market I was telling you about

takes place here,' said Tom indicating the cobblestones in front of the café. 'If we've time tomorrow we should come. They have some great food stalls. I sometimes bring Laura for a day trip and she loves it here.'

'I thought you always called Gran Mrs Potts,' Ellie commented.

'Only to get a rise out of her. I think of her as Laura. She's been great to me, very supportive.' Tom put his menu down. 'What are you having?'

'I'll have the full English. I'm starving.'

'Me too. I'll get us some tea as well — unless you'd prefer coffee.'

'It has to be tea with a fry-up,' Ellie stated.

'Agreed. I'll be back in a sec.'

While she waited for him to order, she watched the square. The cobbled stones at the centre were bordered by small independent shops that were just begging for her to go and search through them. She would do that as soon as she could — hopefully before the end of the day.

Tom had barely sat back down when their breakfasts arrived, the plates stacked high with food. Ellie demolished a rich pork sausage and a thick slice of salty bacon before she considered speaking again.

'I think we should go to the police with what we've got,' she said.

She slathered butter onto a slice of bread while Tom swallowed his mouthful.

'I agree,' he said.

'After we've finished this we'll head over to the local station and tell them everything we know.'

'Will you confess to stealing the key?' Tom asked, a hint of a smile creeping into his voice.

Ellie grinned. 'No, I'll leave that bit out.'

They munched through the rest of their breakfast in comfortable silence. Ellie tried to ignore the thought that he'd make a relaxing boyfriend — but once the idea had popped into her head it was very difficult to shut it back down.

'How's your thesis going?' he asked, bringing her back to normality.

'Badly,' she said. 'I'd like to think it's because I'm so busy with Gran and this investigation but the truth is I'm not enjoying writing up my findings as much as I enjoyed undertaking the research. I'm obviously a more practical person than I realised.'

'Maybe you should become a private eye,' Tom suggested mischievously. 'You're good at it.'

Ellie laughed. She liked the idea as a romantic proposition but it wasn't a serious consideration. With no practical experience of solving crime, she hadn't really a hope in making a business like that work. She was better off in academia, which she knew well and in which she'd mapped out her whole career path.

After a chaotic childhood of travelling the world, never settling in one place for more than a year, she wanted a stable career. She couldn't change her plan at this stage. Could she?

She stabbed her egg yolk with a slice of crunchy, white toast. The skin broke and the runny yolk quickly spread across her plate. She mopped it while picturing herself in an office looking frantically through case files and shouting down the phone at an unreliable witness. She grinned. It was a lovely fantasy but one which wasn't going to happen. It was too uncertain a prospect.

★　★　★

Tom knew where the police station was from his many visits to the town. He strode ahead confidently while Ellie dawdled behind. After the visit to the station, she was going to pop into some of the boutiques. She'd seen the perfect pair of autumn boots to add to her collection and wanted to get a better look.

The police station was tiny. A young officer was sitting behind the reception desk, his eyes on a computer screen and his hand unmoving on a mouse, the epitome of someone trying to look busy while having nothing to do. His eyes lit up as he saw them approach; they may well have been the first people to turn up all day.

Ellie explained to the officer why they were there — and from then on the day dragged.

They were asked to wait before they were taken through a series of questions. Then they were made to wait some more. At one point Tom nodded off to sleep, his head resting on his hand, which was propped up by his elbow. He woke sharply when his elbow gave way and his head plummeted towards his chest. Ellie restrained herself from laughing out loud at his puzzled expression but only just.

It was late afternoon before they left the station. Ellie was drained and viciously hungry.

'Well, that went . . . slowly,' remarked Tom.

'Yeah,' said Ellie sighing. 'It wasn't the best but hopefully we got the message to the right people. Are you hungry?' she asked.

'Amazingly, yes. I thought that breakfast would keep me fed for days but that experience has bored me into a ravenous hunger.'

Shall we head back to the square and find a café? We can plan our next move from there.'

'Sounds good to me, especially the food part,' said Tom enthusiastically.

People flowed past them as they meandered back towards the town centre, the heat of the afternoon making them drowsy. Ellie was just craning her neck to see if the gorgeous boots were still on display when Tom yanked her arm and pulled her to face a shop window.

'Ow,' she complained. 'What's going on?'

'Simon Hawley is on the other side of the square,' Tom whispered harshly.

'Then why are we facing this way?'

'Good point,' said Tom and he turned slowly. 'He's still there.'

'OK,' said Ellie, staring at some knitted kittens in the shop window. 'What's he doing?'

'He's reading a newspaper outside a café.'

'Is there a table free near him?'

'Yes, there's one right next to him.'

'OK, let's go,' said Ellie turning and threading her arm through his.

'What's this about?' asked Tom, nodding his head towards their entwined arms.

'We're a couple out to get a late afternoon meal. This is part of our disguise,' said Ellie confidently.

She didn't really know what the arm-holding was all about. It had seemed the most natural thing in the world to link arms and stroll with Tom across the square. She could feel his muscle through his T-shirt and goose bumps formed on her skin where they touched. She had an urge to squeeze his arm, but she let go instead. Tom was right; there was no reason to hold on to him.

The seats around the table nearest Simon remained empty and Ellie took the closest one to him. Tom sat opposite her and they opened their menus in silence. They ordered and then Ellie took out her phone and pretended to scroll through its screens. Tom did the same. Their drinks of water came and Ellie downed hers in one and ordered another. By the time their meals had arrived, all they'd heard from Simon's table was the rustle of newspaper as he turned the pages.

Ellie picked at her omelette. Her hunger had retreated when they'd caught sight of Simon and her stomach was in a tight knot of anxiety. By the looks of things Tom was feeling the same.

After what felt like an eternity Ellie pushed the last piece of omelette into her mouth. She was halfway through chewing her mouthful when a phone rang, loud and shrill right behind her.

She jumped and spluttered inelegantly.

'Pete!' boomed Simon. 'How are you doing, mate?'

There was silence while Pete responded.

'Are we still on for tonight?'

More silence.

'Excellent, see you at seven.'

Ellie heard the scrape of the chair as Simon stood. She just had time to turn quickly before he disappeared in the throng of people.

'Do you think that was him arranging the next hit?' asked Tom, a little breathlessly.

'It's possible,' Ellie conceded. 'From what you saw of Simon, do you think he's the silhouette from the warehouse yesterday?'

'I can't be certain, but nothing about his physical appearance ruled him out either.'

'OK, here's my suggestion. Stop me if you think I'm being crazy. We don't know where Simon's going but we know where the animals will end up.'

'You want us to stake out the warehouse?' Tom said, catching up with her thought process.

'Yes, but it is a crazy suggestion. We don't really know what he's up to this evening.'

'He could be meeting this Pete guy for a pint,' Tom pointed out.

'Exactly.'

'We've come this far. Let's risk it. If we spend the night watching an empty warehouse, so be it,' said Tom, a gleam of excitement lighting up his eyes.

Ellie looked at her lap for a moment and smoothed her dress absent-mindedly.

'Do you think Pete could be Peter?' she asked quietly.

Tom nodded, 'He could be,' he said sadly. 'But I've never heard anyone call him Pete, it's always Peter. We mustn't assume.'

'No,' said Ellie softly. 'We mustn't assume.'

'Right,' said Tom pushing back the chair, 'what do we need to do to get ready for this stake-out?'

'Let's head back to the hotel and try and get a couple of hours' rest. We'll pick up some food and drinks. Some blankets are a good idea because the temperature will drop in the early hours. We need fully charged phones as well.'

Ellie followed Tom slowly back to the car. Even though it was her suggestion to watch the warehouse, she was starting to regret the move. On one hand, it could be a completely pointless and exhausting effort. On the other hand if they caught Peter in the act tonight, then they'd have to report it to the police and any chance of Charlotte marrying her childhood sweetheart this summer would be over. Neither option was preferable.

* * *

Back at the hotel, she tried to sleep but the room was so hot she couldn't settle. She opted for a long shower under the delicious rain head instead. It cooled her down, but she didn't feel rested by the time she pulled on her jeans and T-shirt.

She picked up her rucksack and shoved in a couple of bottles of water and several energy bars. The hotel wardrobe had a few spare blankets stacked on a shelf. She took two and added them to her bag. She scooped up her jumper from the bed and checked she had her mobile phone. When she decided she had everything she needed, she headed towards the bedroom door. She was ready.

She found Tom was sitting in the bar reading through a discarded newspaper, his own rucksack by his feet.

'Hey,' she said.

He looked up and folded the paper.

'Hey,' he said back. 'Do you need to get anything else or are you ready to go?'

'I'm ready,' she said, fiddling with a strap on her bag.

'Are you sure you want to do this?' asked Tom.

'Yes,' she said, more decisively than she felt. 'Let's go.'

* * *

Without discussing it they left Tom's car in the same office car park they'd used the evening before. The sun was just setting as they made their way over to the warehouses. Ellie held her breath as they crept past the Portakabin but they needn't have worried. They made it past the reception unchallenged.

'Probably still watching the wrestling,' commented Tom.

They'd decided against waiting inside the warehouse.

'It's too smelly,' reasoned Ellie.

'And we don't want to get trapped in a room with angry cows,' pointed out Tom.

They set up camp to the side of a warehouse slightly up the road from warehouse C. Tom spread a blanket on the ground and they both sat down with their backs against the building.

Hours passed and the sun set completely. The air came alive with moths fluttering around them and bats swooping overhead. Ellie closed her eyes for a moment and woke sometime later with her head on Tom's chest and his arm around her shoulders. It had been so long since she'd been held by a man that she'd forgotten what it was like to feel comfort and protection from someone else. She stayed there for a moment enjoying the warmth of his body before pulling herself upright. His arm loosened but stayed around her.

'Anything happening?' she whispered.

'Yes, they've been and gone, but I was enjoying listening to you snore so I just let them get away with it.'

'Ha, very funny. Nothing's changed then?'

'No.'

'Would you like a biscuit bar?' she asked.

'Yes please.'

She leaned forward to reach into her

bag and his arm dropped. She missed his warmth immediately and wondered what she could do to get the arm back.

'Ellie,' said Tom.

She turned and looked at him, his face hovered above hers for a moment.

'There is something I wanted . . . ' he began.

'That is, to say . . . '

Ellie frowned. Tom wasn't known for being hesitant. He ran his hands over his face and took a deep breath.

'I . . . '

Whatever it was he wanted to talk about was cut off when Tom's phone started to ring, the noise sounding shrill in the quiet night air.

'What on earth . . . ?' he said, diving into his rucksack. 'Who could be phoning at this time of night?'

Ellie glanced at her watch. It was just coming up to one o'clock in the morning.

'Mum,' said Tom urgently. 'What's wrong?'

Ellie's heart pounded.

'I'll be right there,' he said and shut the phone down.

'What's happened?' asked Ellie.

Tom was standing and shoving everything back into his rucksack.

'Someone tried to break into my farm this evening and now Dad's hurt. Mum's on her way to the hospital with him. I need to go and be with them.'

12

Ellie woke to the distant ringing of Gran's telephone. One minute she was unconscious, arms flung above her head and her mouth slightly open, and the next she was throwing herself out of bed and running down the stairs. She burst into the kitchen.

'Is there any news?' she demanded.

'Yes, love,' said Gran, replacing the handset in the cradle, 'and it's good. Why don't you sit down next to me and I'll tell you all about it.'

Ellie snuggled into her favourite sofa and pulled a pale blue, knitted throw around her shoulders. The air was warm but Gran had made this throw long before Ellie was born and snuggling into it brought her comfort.

Gran reached out and tugged Ellie towards her. Ellie allowed herself to be pulled into a loving embrace and she settled her head on Gran's shoulder. She inhaled her familiar floral scent and tried to relax.

Tom's frantic drive through the night had left her feeling fraught and strung out. He'd barely stopped to drop her off before shooting off to the hospital to meet his mother. Ellie was desperate to know whether the tall, friendly man she remembered so vividly from her childhood was seriously injured.

'That was Tom on the phone,' Gran said, stroking Ellie's hair off her face. 'I'll start at the end and tell you that everyone is fine so you don't need to worry. The hospital kept Tom's father in because they thought he might have concussion but he's fine. They were also worried about his leg but he's got a bad sprain, no broken bones.'

Ellie let out a shuddering sigh of relief. Last night they'd had no information and she'd feared the worst. Tom must have felt the same.

They hadn't said a word to each other from the time they'd left the warehouse until he'd dropped her off. She'd asked him to call her with news as she'd stepped out of the car. He'd barely paused to agree before he'd driven off into the dark leaving her alone.

'What happened at the farm?' Ellie asked.

'Tom's parents were asleep when Tilly started growling. Lynn's a light sleeper so she woke first and got up to see what was wrong with her. Tilly's not normally a growler and at first Lynn thought Tilly was missing Tom. She tried to coax her up to their bedroom but Tilly wasn't having it. She wouldn't move from the front door and her growls were getting more aggressive. No one's ever seen an aggressive Tilly before.

'Lynn went to wake Tom's dad and from their bedroom window they could just make out what appeared to be a dark van parked in front of Tom's gate. Lynn wanted to call the police straight away but Tom's dad decided to go out and investigate.'

'Tom will be cross,' said Ellie. 'He made his parents promise they wouldn't go out and confront any would be thieves.'

'I don't think he was planning to confront them, love. His plan, or so he says, was to sneak up close to whoever was there and try to identify them. He took his phone with him and he was going to take some photos.'

Ellie grimaced. 'His phone camera wouldn't have worked well in the dark. The resolution would have been terrible. Or worse, there would have been a huge flash and he'd have been spotted straight away. In a way, it was a good job he fell. It would have been worse if the thieves had seen him; they may have done some real damage.'

Ellie saw Gran's face; perhaps her reaction had been a little harsh. 'His plan didn't go well, then?' she said, softening her voice.

'No. In the darkness he tripped and fell, banging his head and damaging his ankle. In the confusion that followed the intruder got away.'

'Did either of them see a number plate?' Ellie asked.

'No. There was a lot of blood from the head wound. Lynn was frightened and panicking and didn't pay any attention to the van and its driver.'

'Head wounds do bleed a lot,' said Ellie contemplatively.

'They're convinced someone was there, though there was no supporting evidence,' said Gran.

Ellie nodded and cuddled in closer. For a while they sat in silence, Gran gently stroking Ellie's hair.

'Is Tom's dad staying in hospital?' Ellie asked after a while.

'No, he's been released. They're all going back to the farm so Tom can help his mum out. I offered to bring them some food and so Tom's invited us both around tomorrow evening for an evening meal. I'll take some of my pre-made stew but I'd be grateful if you could prepare some fresh vegetables.'

Ellie nodded. 'Of course I can. Do I need to go out or have we got enough in?'

'Andrew and I went shopping earlier. We've loads of food,' said Gran. 'When you've recovered a bit, perhaps you could tell me about your trip to Boxcomb.'

'I'll tell you all about it now. I'll make us a cup of tea first, shall I?'

'Yes please, dear. Oh, and if you check in the red tin by the sink you should find some chocolate brownies. Charlotte dropped them off yesterday morning. She said you seemed to particularly enjoy them when you two met up for a chat at The Café by the Sea so when she was in there yesterday, she bought some more for you.'

'Gosh, that was kind of her. She's right about me loving them, the cook at that café is a goddess,' said Ellie, making straight for the red tin.

She tugged on the lid and inhaled the rich aroma of thick chocolate. She cut two generous pieces and stuck them, literally, on two of Gran's flowery porcelain plates.

'I think you're going to love this,' she said, handing Gran her piece.

'Oh, wow,' said Gran after taking her first bite. 'This is heaven on a plate.'

Emily laughed and popped a large mug of tea on the side table nearest Gran's arm. Settling back on the settee next to her she said, 'Let's wait until we've finished the cake before we talk about my weekend. I don't want anything to spoil our enjoyment of chocolate paradise.'

They ate in a silence only broken by the occasional moan of delight. Every mouthful was divine. Ellie was going to have to ask Gran to send her brownies from The Café by the Sea in the post when she returned to London. She didn't know how she would get by without these cakes in her life.

When they'd finished and mopped up every last crumb Ellie took their plates and put them in the sink.

'I'm pretty sure we can rule Andrew

out of our list of suspects,' she said as the plates plopped silently into the water. She wiped them over with a dishcloth and then turned to look at Gran who'd remained silent after her statement.

Gran was nodding silently and looking out at the garden through the kitchen window. To Ellie's horror she realised tears were sneaking down Gran's face.

'Gran,' said Ellie her voice tremulous. 'Why are you crying?'

She rushed to Gran's side and slid her arms around Gran's waist holding her tight.

'Ignore me,' said Gran her voice croaky. 'I'm being silly. It's just such a relief to know that you don't think Andrew's behind the crimes. I never thought he was, but if he had been I don't know how the community would have come back from him being responsible for the attacks on Roger and Tom. Now,' said Gran more firmly as she wiped her eyes vigorously, 'tell me why you've come to that conclusion.'

Ellie sat back down, tucked her feet under her legs and turned to face her grandmother.

'It was this warehouse we found . . . '

She told Gran everything she and Tom had done since they'd left Morwenna Bay on Friday morning until they had returned in the early hours of this morning. Even though Ellie had slept for most of the morning, she still felt exhausted by the time she finished relaying her news.

'Did the police get back to you to say whether the warehouse had been accessed after you left last night?'

'Not yet,' said Ellie. 'I'm not sure they would get in contact with me either way. I only phoned the warehouse connection in on our way home last night but it's not as if I personally have a vested interest in whether or not the warehouse was used.'

'You could always phone your good friend from the warehouse, David

Banks,' Gran suggested.

'Good idea,' said Ellie, digging her mobile out of her dressing gown pocket.

David answered on the second ring and was very pleased to hear from her. He was clearly enjoying the excitement the case was bringing to his otherwise dull job.

'The police stayed for the rest of the night but no one turned up with a truckload of animals,' Ellie told Gran when she got off the phone.

'Did David ask for his key back?'

'No, he doesn't seem to have noticed I've still got it. I don't think security is his strong point,' said Ellie, smiling. 'I'm not sure it will do us any good now. If the thief caught wind of the police presence at the warehouse last night, then I'd be surprised if he returned. I'll post it back to him apologising for my mistake.'

'Apart from deciding that Andrew isn't guilty, have you come to any further conclusions?'

'I think we seriously need to consider that Peter is involved somehow. I know that both he and Charlotte seem lovely but the evidence is stacking up against him.' said Ellie sadly.

Gran nodded her expression grim.

'He has several strikes against him. Firstly,' Ellie ticked points off on her fingers, 'he's come into some wealth recently. I saw The Westerly when I was in Boxcomb and to say it's luxurious is an understatement. I made a flippant comment about them being able to afford Claridges but this hotel must be on a par financially.'

'I can't see where else he'd be getting the money from,' Gran said resignedly.

'Secondly, there's Simon Hawley agreeing to meet a man named Pete on the same night Tom's farm is attacked. Thirdly, we know he's worked as a farmhand so he would have knowledge of all the farms locally, including their routines, and he'd know how to keep the animals calm while getting them on transporters.'

Gran nodded.

'And the final point — and I don't have any proof of this, it's just a guess — is that he knew Tom was going to be away this weekend.'

'How could he know?' Gran challenged.

'I told Charlotte,' Ellie stated baldly.

'Oh,' said Gran.

Ellie leaned on Gran and closed her eyes.

'The thing is, I really like Charlotte, Gran. I don't want to be the one to spoil the happiness she's waited her lifetime to achieve.'

13

'Have you got everything?' Gran asked anxiously. 'You've asked me that a thousand times. I have everything!' said Ellie exasperatedly. She opened the boot of the taxi and started loading the bags and boxes into it. 'You'd swear we were going away for a week, not just for an evening meal,' she muttered.

'We are staying the night as well,' said Gran as another bag went into the boot.

'I know,' said Ellie, keener than she'd admit about seeing inside Tom's house. She'd been glad when Lynn had suggested they stay over so they wouldn't have to deal with getting Gran home after drinking wine. 'It's just we seem to be taking more for one night than I packed for my entire stay at your house.'

The taxi driver grinned at her. 'Is there any room for this?' he asked, indicating Gran's chair.

'It can go in the back seat with me,' said Ellie as she loaded the last of the bags and shut the boot.

After lots of manoeuvring and quite a few bad words, the wheelchair was secured in the back and they were ready to go.

It was years since Ellie had been to Tom's farm. In her mind the place was always bathed in sunshine. People came in and out of focus but her main recollections were always about the animals. Sows so fat it was a miracle they could move, with piglets scurrying around hungrily. Cows eating constantly, flies drawn to their faces, their udders plump with milk. She'd fallen in love with whatever baby animal she'd found. She'd seen them all, ducklings, kittens, piglets but her favourites were always the puppies. Several times over the years she'd seen the puppies born from the farm's sheepdogs. Once she'd fallen desperately in love with a gorgeous bitch with a patch of white fur around her left eye.

She'd nagged and nagged her parents to allow her to take the puppy home but they'd refused. Their lifestyle wasn't suitable, always moving from city to city. Busy with work. It would be cruel to keep a dog in those circumstances. The young Ellie had promised herself she would get a dog when she was older but the reality was that her parents were right. Lifestyle and work got in the way of keeping a dog.

To keep a dog now would be unkind. She'd never see it because she was always working and it would be cooped up in her tiny flat all day, alone.

It was such a short drive to Tom's farmhouse that in normal circumstances they would have walked. But Ellie would never have made it through the winding country roads with Gran in her chair, and with all the food and luggage Gran had decided they needed for just one evening.

Ellie's heartbeat picked up as they neared the gates to Tom's farmhouse.

'You're looking a little flushed, dear. Are you all right?' asked Gran, who'd twisted round in the front seat to look at her.

'I'm fine. It's a bit hot in here, that's all,' she replied, unsure as to why her heart was beating faster and her face was getting hotter. 'I'm looking forward to seeing all the animals,' she said quickly to distract Gran from pointing out that the car had excellent air conditioning and that it was, in fact, quite cool.

'You do know Tom only farms cows these days?' asked Gran. 'It's not like when his parents had the farm and they had a little of everything.'

'I thought he still had pigs,' Ellie commented as the taxi swung round the large courtyard at the centre of Tom's farm and came to a stop.

'Well, yes, but they're kept as pets rather than farmed.'

'And I can see ducks over there,' Ellie continued.

'Yes, but they're wild and just come

to the pond when they feel like it.'

'Then there's Tilly,' said Ellie.

Gran sighed and stopped talking.

Ellie hopped out of the car as a tall lady, her ash-blonde hair fading to grey, stepped out of the front door.

'Lynn,' called Ellie, striding across to the woman whom she hadn't seen in years but who was so familiar to her.

'Ellie,' said Lynn, holding out her arms and enveloping her young visitor in a big hug. 'It's so lovely to see you again after all this time.' She held Ellie at arm's length. 'And you've grown so pretty. I knew you would.'

'Don't forget about me,' called Gran, who was still in the taxi.

'Come on then, Laura, let's get you out and into the house,' said Lynn, laughing at her friend.

As Gran was getting more mobile and able to help with the manoeuvring, Lynn was able to hoist Laura out of the car and into the wheelchair by herself. Ellie paid the driver and collected the bags from the boot.

'Gosh,' said Lynn, 'you have brought a lot.'

'That's what I said,' said Ellie, laughing at Gran's expression. Gran clearly believed that a suitcase was a reasonable amount of luggage for one night's stay.

Weighed down by bags she followed the two ladies into the house. Tilly greeted them madly as they stepped inside; barking and spinning in circles. Lynn laughed and tried to push her out of the way but Tilly was immovable until she'd covered all of Gran's and Ellie's unclothed bits of skin in licks. After she'd achieved her goal she was content to follow the women deeper into the house.

Although Ellie's memories of the farm were vivid, she had few recollections of the farmhouse itself. She could remember the kitchen because Lynn always tugged her in and fed her cake or biscuits whenever she wandered over, but maybe she'd never ventured into the rest of the house, because she felt she was seeing it all for the first time. Or maybe it was the curiosity of seeing where Tom lived.

The hallway was painted a pale grey and the only decoration was a large painting of Morwenna Bay on the left wall. Unless he'd had a major tidy up in honour of their arrival, and Ellie couldn't see when Tom would have had the time, he was a lot tidier than her. Her flat's hallway was full of shoes, coats and bags, dumped there after a long day at work, that she hadn't found the time or inclination to clear up later.

She followed Lynn and Gran down the narrow hallway which opened up into a wide lounge.

'Wow,' said Ellie as she caught sight of the view from floor-to-ceiling windows, 'it's stunning in here.'

'You're too kind,' said a deep voice from the middle of a corner sofa which curved around the back wall and faced the large windows.

'I think she meant the view,' said Lynn, 'not you, you big lump.'

'Oh, Thomas,' said Gran who caught sight of Tom's dad sitting on the sofa at the same time as Ellie. A dramatic bandage was wound around his head and his ankle was propped up on a footstool. 'You look dreadful.'

'From stunning to dreadful in less than thirty seconds, that's quite a comedown,' he said, the twinkle in his blue eyes so like his son's. 'Hello, Ellie, it's lovely to see you again after so long. Why don't you come and sit next to me and tell me all about your life since we last saw you. Lynn and Tom can see to the meal.'

'Yes, you sit down, Ellie,' said Lynn, taking the bags from her and nudging her towards the sofa. 'He's been as grumpy as a bear all day because we've forced him to sit down and rest. Take his mind off it by telling him all about your adventures. Laura, I'll take you into the kitchen so you can talk to me while I put this delicious-looking food together.'

Ellie settled on the soft sofa, moving

215

carefully so she didn't jolt the leg wrapped in bandages. Tilly settled on her feet, letting out a sigh of contentment as she rested her head on the floor.

Ellie took her time to take in her surroundings, trying to deduce more about Tom's character from the lounge's contents. Like the hall, it was neat and apart from the long sofa and an oak coffee table, it was sparse on furniture. She glanced at Tom's dad; he was watching her evaluate the room with an amused twinkle. Realising she'd been caught snooping she asked the first thing that came into her head.

'Does it get confusing,' she asked, 'with you and Tom having the same name?'

'When we're together most people call Dad Big Tom,' said Tom coming into the room with a large glass of wine for Ellie and a glass of water for his father.

Ellie nodded and smiled up at Tom,

thanking him as he handed her the glass.

'Big on account of his massive stomach,' added Tom with a quick wink in Ellie's direction.

'Hey,' said Big Tom, 'that is absolutely not true. I'm Big Tom because overall I'm manlier than that little one over there. A fact I'd prove to you if I was able to stand.'

'I think the fact you're not able to stand proves my point, Dad,' said Tom laughing.

At the sight of Tom's smile Ellie's heart did a strange little jump and her heart rate picked up again. This was getting ridiculous. Tom was Tearaway Tom, for goodness sake, the sullen boy always dressed in black. She'd known him since forever. She was not going to get all moony-eyed over a smile. It was frustrating that she had to keep reminding herself of that.

'How are you feeling?' she asked Big Tom, taking her attention away from his son.

'Grumpy,' said Tom, answering on behalf of his dad.

'I'm feeling perfectly well, thank you, Ellie,' said Big Tom. 'You can ignore my son. I have been nothing but courteous all day.'

Tom snorted. 'Don't you believe it. I'd better go and help Mum in the kitchen. Shout if you need rescuing, Ellie.'

They made for an odd bunch, sitting around a large dining table. With Gran and her massive leg cast and Big Tom's huge bandage wrapped around his head, they looked as if they'd been in a huge fight and lost. Ellie had worried that the conversation would be all doom and gloom about the attacks on the farms, but these were only mentioned briefly. The rest of the conversation flowed smoothly as they ate through Gran's pre-prepared Irish stew.

Perhaps, thought Ellie, she should get some cooking lessons from her gran before she returned to London. Her idea of preparing food was to stab a packet with a fork and to shove it in a microwave. Gran had outdone herself this evening with lamb shoulder slow-cooked with smoked bacon, shallots and mushrooms in a rich sauce, served with the fresh vegetables Ellie had spent the morning preparing.

Ellie could manage a basic pudding, and tonight she'd made her favourite dessert using rhubarb she'd found growing in Gran's garden and adding a sweet crumble topping with crunchy oats and sprinkled with sugar. Lynn had just served it up with dollops of vanilla ice cream when Gran started to yawn theatrically.

'Do you want me to help you get ready for bed, Gran?' asked Ellie.

'No need to call an end to the evening just yet, Ellie,' boomed Big Tom. 'Why don't you and Tom head down to the pub for a drink while us old folk have a nightcap? We can help Laura to bed.'

'Good idea, Dad,' said Tom pushing

back his chair and standing up. 'We'll go now. Come on, Ellie.'

Before Ellie even had time to form an opinion she and Tom were out of the front door and on their way to The Ship.

'Shouldn't we have helped clear up?' asked Ellie as they all but sprinted down the road towards the village centre.

Tom laughed. 'I think,' he said, 'that we should take advantage of the fact that my parents and your Gran are trying to set us up to get out of the washing-up.'

Ellie walked in silence for a moment.

'Gran promised me she wasn't trying to set us up,' she said eventually.

'Maybe it's just my parents, then. A few of Mum's friends have had grandchildren recently and Mum's been making subtle hints that she'd like some of her own. I did point out that I needed a girlfriend first and it looks as if they've decided you'd make an excellent choice. Not only are you from a good family but your gran's land runs alongside mine. In their eyes it's a perfect match. It could also be that Laura wasn't entirely truthful with you. I'm pretty sure that reference she made during dinner as to how much I'd enjoy Wimbledon's fiery food festival was a hint for you to invite me to stay with you while it's on.'

'She is unbelievable!' said Ellie incredulously.

Tom laughed at her indignation.

'I've never taken my parents advice on my love life before so let's forget about and enjoy the evening,' he suggested.

'Actually I've had an idea about this evening,' said Ellie.

'Oh?'

'About the case, not about us,' said Ellie hurriedly in case he got the wrong idea.

'OK,' said Tom.

Ellie wasn't sure but she thought he sounded disappointed. Still, he'd more or less just told her he wasn't interested in her in that way, so she must have misinterpreted his voice.

'Who knew you were going away last weekend?' she asked, deciding to focus solely on the case from now on. A resolution she kept making and breaking whenever she was around Tom.

'A few people. I probably mentioned it when I was down the pub one evening last week. I have no idea exactly who would have known.'

'Did you tell anyone why you were going away?' Ellie asked.

'Not outside of my immediate family, no. I didn't mention you were coming away with me either. I've not mentioned Laura's investigation to anyone. I thought it could create bad feeling with villagers if they thought we might suspect them of a crime they haven't committed.'

Ellie nodded. 'I agree that we should keep the investigation to ourselves. OK, so let's imagine for a moment that the person or people who came to your farm two nights ago knew you were going to be away because they heard it either from you or from me.

'OK,' said Tom slowly.

'Why don't we, while we're at the pub tonight, play down what happened to your dad?'

'Why mention it at all?' Tom asked.

'The thief disappeared after your dad fell, so we can assume that he saw some movement or heard a noise, which convinced him he'd be caught if he stayed. We pretend your dad saw nothing untoward.'

'OK, then what?'

'Do you always have someone staying at the farm while you're away?' Ellie asked.

'I hardly ever go away but my parents would normally stay over if I did. Obviously they're the best people to call as they have all the experience looking after animals and I trust them completely.'

'Is it believable that you'd go away for the night and not have someone stay over to keep an eye on the farm?' Ellie asked.

'Not really — although the thief didn't seem to think so on Saturday.'

'Whoever it was is going to be more cautious now that they know someone was there while you were in Boxcomb,' said Ellie.

'What is it that you're planning?'

'We could tell people we're going to see the Haf festival in Cardiff in two weeks' time. It runs over the whole weekend so we'd be away for at least two days, possibly three. So that we get the message across to everyone local, we could ask around for recommendations on places to stay. Oh, and we could specify that we want a place that allows dogs to stay because we want to take Tilly with us. That rules out Tilly acting as a guard dog. It lets people know we're going to be away without being too obvious. What do you think?'

'The plan sounds OK so far, but then what?'

'Maybe we could say that Roger is

going to look after the farm for you because your dad can't do it with his damaged leg and your mum can't leave him home alone. That might relax any would-be thief. They've got past Roger once before so they must think they can do it again. On the day of the festival Roger could come up with a reason as to why he won't be there but he's not able to get hold of you to let you know. Obviously we won't go to the festival. Instead we lie in wait and see if the thief strikes again. It's a long shot but it's all we have at the moment.'

'OK, I see your thinking. But isn't it a little odd that we're going to this festival together?'

'Everyone seems to think we're on our way to becoming a couple. Let's make it believable.'

'I can get on board with that,' said Tom with a grin.

'We'd best make sure our families are in on the plan. We don't want Gran and Lynn to start knitting baby bonnets.'

Tom barked out a laugh as they

arrived at the doors to The Ship.

Ellie took a deep breath and laced her fingers with Tom's. His hand was warm and firm. It was time to make it seem believable that they were more than friends.

'Ellie,' said Tom tightening his fingers on her hand to stop her opening the door to the pub.

'Yes,' she said looking up at him. She couldn't read the expression on his face, she thought he might look sad, but she couldn't think why that would be.

'Are you sure you want to do this?' he asked. 'You've done enough for us. We could leave the rest of the investigation to the police and no one would think any less of you. Please don't do something that makes you feel uncomfortable.'

Ellie squeezed his fingers.

'You're not making me do anything I don't want to do,' she said. 'I want to know who's behind this, especially after tonight and seeing your dad with that massive bandage.

'Your dad was so kind to me when I was younger. He was patient with me when he could have chucked me off the farm and told me to stop bothering him. I saw more of him during my summers here than I did of my own father, who was so busy flying from country to country on business that I hardly spent any time with him.'

Tom nodded and drew her into the bustling pub.

'You always seemed so exotic to me when we were younger,' he said as they made their way to the bar through the throng. 'You'd seen more of the world by the time you were ten than I have now. At that age the furthest I'd been was Tenby.'

'Tenby's lovely,' said Ellie, thinking of a week she'd spent at the seaside town with her grandparents years ago. She could still vividly remember the wide open beaches and the smell of the fish and chips they'd eaten while overlooking the water. She'd probably enjoyed her time there more than any of the far-flung holidays her parents had taken her on, when they'd expected her to be on her best behaviour as they visited museum after museum. Tenby had been much more fun.

'True, but Tenby isn't Dubai, is it?' commented Tom, breaking in on her thoughts.

Ellie laughed and caught sight of Mike watching them with a frown.

She turned to Tom. 'Why's Mike looking so cross?' she asked.

'Ah,' said Tom. 'I think he was hoping to ask you out himself. He's probably spotted us holding hands and is angry with me for stealing a march on him.'

'I guess that means my free drinks are off the menu,' said Ellie with mock sadness.

Tom laughed. 'I doubt it. Mike's generous. He'll only hold a grudge for a few minutes. Besides you'll be gone in a few weeks and when he sees me broken-hearted he'll think he's made a lucky escape.'

Tom grinned at her, reassuring her

that he wouldn't really mind when she disappeared from his life and then he turned to order some drinks from the barmaid. Ellie looked back towards the pub owner. Sure enough his frown had gone and he was making his way over to them.

'Ellie,' Mike said cheerfully. 'You've finally made it down.'

'I'm sorry I missed tapas night again, Mike. I was away for the weekend. Tom took me to see Boxcomb and we stayed a couple of nights.'

'Did you have a good time?' Mike asked.

'It was very relaxing — well, it was until we had to rush back in the dead of night. Tom's dad fell and hurt himself,' she explained.

'What happened? Is he all right?' Mike asked his brow furrowing.

'He was staying at the farm and thought he heard a noise outside. He went out to investigate and fell. He's got a bad sprain and a sore head,' said Ellie, 'but otherwise he's fine.'

'It was all very dramatic over nothing,' said Tom, handing Ellie a large glass of wine. 'We're all a bit spooked since Roger's and Andrew's farms were attacked. Dad will be up and about soon. You know what he's like.'

'I'm pleased to hear it. Don't pay for those,' said Mike gesturing to the barmaid to return Tom's money to him. 'I've been promising Ellie free drinks since she got here.'

'Thanks, Mike,' said Ellie, glad that Mike was going to continue with his friendly approach. She wouldn't have agreed to go on a date if he'd asked, but that was down to her not wanting a relationship with anyone at the moment and not because he wasn't a good-looking, friendly guy.

'Did Big Fish play here on Friday?' Tom asked Mike.

'Yes, they did. They were great. I'm hoping to have them again over the summer.'

'I think they're playing at the Haf

festival in Cardiff. Ellie and I are planning to go so hopefully we can see them there.'

Mike raised his eyebrows, 'It's not like you to spend so much time away from the farm.'

'Ellie's not going to be around for much longer. I'm making the most of things while she's here,' said Tom, grinning at Ellie. 'I'll have to have someone else at the farm though. I don't think Dad's going to be up for it any time soon.'

Tom was being about as subtle as a bulldozer but he was getting the message across. They just had to hope that Mike was indiscreet enough to tell anyone who'd listen.

'I've just seen Charlotte,' Ellie told Tom. 'I'm going to pop over and say hi.'

She left the two men to chat and made her way across the pub to Charlotte, saying hello to a few of the Lavender Ladies she recognised along the way. With any luck she'd be able to turn the conversation with Charlotte around to the festival easily. If not, she was going to have to be as subtle as Tom. It didn't matter about the method so long as Peter found out they were going to be away that weekend.

After two more glasses of free wine and a lot of talking about the festival to everyone she spoke to, Tom came over to find her.

'We'd better head back,' said Tom.

'OK,' said Ellie, standing and feeling the room reel slightly. Perhaps she'd taken a bit too much advantage of the free wine.

After saying goodbye to all her new friends she happily tucked her arm into Tom's and allowed herself to be guided out of the pub. The night air was refreshing and she sighed contentedly, leaning into Tom's side.

'I think we can safely say everyone knows about our trip to the festival,' said Tom as they wove their way back to his farmhouse. 'Just telling Mike was probably enough. He's the local gossip and it will be juicy news that I'm dating

Laura Potts' granddaughter. Tomorrow we won't be able to move for everyone knowing about it.'

'I told everyone,' Ellie chirped happily. 'Everyone's been so enthusiastic about the festival and the places we should stay and the bands we should watch. I almost wish we were really going.'

'You seem to have made a lot of friends this evening,' Tom commented, amused.

'Yes, everyone was so lovely. I had such a lovely time. Hey, what are you grinning at?'

'Nothing,' said Tom smiling even wider.

'Do you think I'm tipsy?' demanded Ellie.

'Of course not!'

'Maybe I am just a little but only to the extent that everything in the world seems wonderful.'

Tom chuckled quietly and pulled her closer to him. They walked for a while in contented silence.

'Are you going to tell me who your crush was on then?' she asked, out of the blue.

'Nope,' said Tom.

'Why won't you tell me?' Ellie whined.

Tom grinned. 'Mainly because it's bugging you not to know.'

'I know who it was,' exclaimed Ellie, stopping and pulling her arm out from Tom's. 'It was me, wasn't it? There's no need to keep it from me otherwise. I don't know anyone in the village.'

She started bouncing on the balls of her feet and clapping her hands excitedly. She'd definitely had one too many.

Tom sighed and rolled his eyes.

'Yes, all right, it was you. Happy now?'

'Yay,' said Ellie and slipped her arm back through his.

They walked in silence for a moment with Ellie grinning and Tom watching her, amusement shining from his eyes.

'Why are you so pleased about it?' he

asked. 'You don't even remember me from that time.'

'It's exciting. The young me thought I was very unattractive. I wish I could travel back in time and tell her that someone liked her enough to do something daft enough as to dress all in black to attract her attention. It would have done a lot for her self-esteem.'

Tom stopped them and looked down at her. 'There is no way you can ever have thought you were unattractive. You're beautiful.'

'Thank you for that, but I've always felt uncomfortable in my own skin. I'm so tall; I've never felt anything other than the lanky kid everyone stares at. My parents travelled so much that I was always starting a new school and feeling like the odd kid. Boys didn't want to date the weirdo. I didn't have a boyfriend until I was at university and I was nineteen.'

Tom brushed some hair from her face.

'I think all those boys were cowards

who were too intimidated to speak to the prettiest girl in the school.'

Ellie scoffed.

'It's true, you're beautiful. I've always thought so. You'd come here every summer with your well-travelled sophistication and your highly inappropriate footwear and then one summer, when we were both thirteen, bam, from out of nowhere I was hit with this debilitating crush.'

'Did we ever even speak?'

Tom laughed. 'I was too in awe to speak to you. The only time you spoke to me was when you tried to enlist my help to steal one of my father's Border collie puppies.'

'I remember the dog — she was so gorgeous with a little white patch over one eye. I've never wanted a dog as badly as I wanted her. I still dream about her sometimes. I don't remember you being involved at all, though. Did you help me?'

'I'm wounded,' Tom said theatrically, placing a hand over his heart. 'It was the highlight of my summer. Yes, of course I helped you. You're forgetting the massive size of my crush. If you'd asked me to steal the entire farm for you I'd have agreed.'

Ellie laughed, 'All I remember is the puppy squirming so much when forced her into my coat pocket that I didn't make it to the gate before I was spotted. I got a right earful but I don't remember you being told off. And — ' said Ellie, suddenly remembering Tom's earlier comment — 'what do you mean by 'inappropriate footwear'?'

'You're wearing heeled suede boots,' Tom pointed out, looking down at her legs in mock despair.

Ellie followed his gaze and looked at her much-loved boots covering her skinny jeans. There was nothing wrong with them as far as she could see.

'These are my current favourites,' she protested. 'What's wrong with them?'

'I can't fault the look of you in them, but suede . . . on a trip to a farm?' He shook his head, smiling down at her.

'You're lucky I keep things in the yard clean, otherwise they'd have been ruined this evening.'

Maybe it was the wine or maybe it was the way Tom was smiling softly at her, but something made Ellie act completely out of character.

She leaned towards Tom and gently pressed her mouth against his.

14

Tom strode across the field back towards the farmhouse with the early summer sun warming his back. He slowed as his home came into view. It all looked peaceful and he wondered if his guests were all still asleep.

His parents, used to a lifetime of early starts, might be up and about but whenever Laura stayed over at his parents' house she wasn't known for rising in a hurry. Ellie was probably sleeping off a mild hangover — unless she'd used his absence to scarper without having to see him.

He smiled grimly and resumed walking briskly towards the house. He'd been mulling over how to act around Ellie since he'd woken up this morning, but he still wasn't any the wiser on the best way to proceed. Instinct told him she wouldn't be happy about what had happened between them last night now that she was sober.

He really wished he'd not told her how beautiful he thought she was. That was bound to have upset her now that she was clear-headed enough to think about it. She'd probably wound herself up during the night imagining he was on the verge of proposing marriage. He snorted. He was going to have to wing it when he was around her this morning.

The smell of frying bacon reached him before he got to his kitchen door. One of the good things about having his parents to stay was the cooked breakfasts. Alone, he made do with a few slices of toast — often eaten cold because he was too busy to stop and sit down to eat.

'Ah, there you are,' said his mum as he pushed open the door. 'I've almost finished cooking breakfast.'

All his guests were up and dressed. Ellie was looking a little pale and was drinking something hot from a large white mug.

'Morning, all. How is everyone today?' Tom asked, overly brightly. He'd need to tone it down a bit otherwise he'd look suspicious.

Everyone responded cheerfully apart from Ellie who smiled politely and studied the contents of her mug intently.

'Did Ellie tell you all her plan for entrapping our local thief?' asked Tom as he pulled out his cutlery drawer and started hunting for the right number of knives and forks.

'She did,' said Laura. 'We're all agreed it's an excellent idea.'

It could have been the worst idea in history but Laura would still love it. Ellie could do no wrong in her eyes.

'We thought we'd all stay here,' added Laura. 'As your back-up.'

Tom could see Ellie shaking her head behind Laura's back. He grinned and winked at her and she smiled wanly back. Oh dear, it looked as if she was seriously regretting last night. He was going to have to play it casually. He didn't want her to freak out and avoid him for the rest of her stay in Wales. Things had just started to get interesting between them.

'Right,' said Tom. 'So will it be you and Dad as a crime-fighting duo, Laura?'

Tom was rewarded for his cheekiness with a small giggle from Ellie.

Laura tilted her head to look at her granddaughter, who'd turned her attention back to the contents of her mug.

'No, you're quite right, that won't do at all,' said Laura after a moment of reflection. 'Do you know, I see your point. There's no reason for us all to be here. Just you and Ellie will be more than enough. Don't you think, Lynn?'

His dad looked like he was about to protest but Lynn shot him down with a glare.

'You're right, Laura,' Lynn said. 'It's best we leave this to you two. We don't want another accident. Laura, you can stay the night with us, if you like. We'll look after you — unless you plan to stay with Andrew again.'

They were so unsubtle they were embarrassing. If they carried on with their heavy-handed matchmaking Ellie would be sprinting for the door.

'Well,' said Tom shrugging nonchalantly. 'It doesn't really matter either way. I've plenty of bedrooms so long as we can agree there'll be no more heroics. Here, Laura, why don't you hand out the cutlery and I'll find us some clean plates?'

★   ★   ★

The conversation at breakfast was mainly between Laura and Lynn who chattered away like birds. Ellie ate in silence, refusing to make eye contact with anyone. If her odd behaviour was noticed by anybody else, no one commented.

'Before you go home today, Ellie,' said Tom when they'd all finished their

243

meals and were sitting drinking coffee, 'I'd like to take you to meet someone.'

'Is it to do with the case?' she asked guardedly.

He took a big gulp of coffee and while swallowing he made an, 'mmm,' type of noise and wobbled his head. This morning's visit was nothing to do with the case but if he confessed to that, she'd be back at her Gran's house before he could say 'sheep rustling'.

'We'll clear up if you want to head off straight away,' said his mum, clearly still holding out for romance.

Ellie put her mug down and stood as if she were about to face the gallows.

They put their shoes on in silence and Tom opened the front door to let her through.

'We'll walk, if that's OK with you,' Tom said.

She nodded miserably.

They headed down his driveway and out into the narrow lanes outside.

'Don't worry,' he said after a few minutes' silence. 'I'm not going to try

244

and start where we left off last night.'

He saw her shoulders clench at his comment and he smiled. Even though this morning was a bit of a dent to his pride, her embarrassment was kind of cute. He hoped she would snap out of it soon; he preferred the woman she'd been last night. After quite a bit of alcohol admittedly, she'd been a different person; relaxed and carefree.

She'd kissed him as they'd meandered slowly home and he'd kissed her back. They'd staggered through his front door, giggling over nothing and then he'd kissed her again before sending her packing to his spare room. He'd hoped, although not expected, that she'd be relaxed this morning but she was clearly having some serious regrets.

'I'm sorry if I gave you the wrong impression last night,' she said, her voice muffled as she pressed her chin against her chest. 'I'm not looking for a relationship right now. My job is . . . '

'Yes, I know,' he said gently. 'You're

concentrating on your career at the moment. Let's not get bogged down in embarrassment about a couple of kisses.'

She nodded, still not looking at him. He sighed. He hoped what he was about to show her would lighten her mood.

They came to a house only a short walk from his farm. He'd called in on the owners earlier to ask if they could visit, so they were expected. He knocked gently on the wooden front door.

'Tom,' said Stuart, his friend, as he opened the door. 'Come in. Hello, Ellie, I believe we're about to reunite you with a long-lost friend.'

Tom saw Ellie frown as Stuart led them through his house and out to his patio. There, curled up and resting in the sunlight was an elderly sheepdog with a white patch around one eye.

'Oh,' said Ellie softly, her hand going to her heart. 'It's . . . ' she said but didn't finish her sentence as the old girl woke up and pulled herself to her feet. She padded softly over to Ellie and began to lick the back of her hand.

'Ah, Betsy remembers you,' said Stuart. 'We'll leave you to get reacquainted. She's not so active these days but she loves a good tummy rub.'

Tom followed Stuart back into the house, only turning once to see Ellie bending over to rub Betsy's stomach. He wasn't sure, but he thought she was crying. Hopefully they were tears of joy otherwise he'd made a serious misjudgment.

He let Ellie have half an hour alone with the dog she'd loved so much when she was a teenager and then he went to find her. Betsy was asleep at Ellie's feet while Ellie ran her fingers slowly through the hair on her back. Her eyes were suspiciously red, but at least now she was making eye contact with him.

'Thanks for bringing me to see Betsy,' she said, giving the dog one last stroke before standing up. 'She's as gorgeous as I remember.'

Tom smiled. 'She's given a lot of joy to Stuart and his family over the years. She's had a happy life. I thought you'd be pleased to see her and to know where she's been all these years.'

Ellie let out a ghost of a laugh. 'I'm really pleased she's had a good life. Far better living here in this lovely garden than in my coat pocket.'

Tom smiled. 'I've got to get back to the farm now,' he said. 'I've got a lot of catching up to do. Stuart's gone out but he said you're welcome back any time to spend a bit of time with Betsy. If you promise not to try and smuggle her away again, you can probably take her for a walk. She enjoys the beach.'

'Thanks, Tom,' said Ellie as they made their way back through the house and onto the lanes leading back to the farm.

'What's next with the case?' he asked, keen to keep her talking and not brooding.

'What did the police say about the possible break-in at your place?' she asked, sounding more like herself.

'Nothing. There was nothing to see, so there was nothing they could do. We can't even prove there was anyone there on Saturday night.'

Ellie nodded slowly. 'I think it's best to leave the investigation until the day of our supposed trip to the festival, then. We've nothing else to go on. You've got lots to do with your farm and I need to concentrate on getting Gran the right support she'll need when I leave. Not to mention more work on my infamous unfinished thesis.'

Ellie's suggested plan didn't allow for them to meet up at any point. He focused on not being too disappointed about that. They'd only met a few weeks ago after half a lifetime of not seeing each other. They were just about friends.

It shouldn't matter to him that she was returning to London less than a week after their entrapment weekend idea. It didn't matter to him; the ache in his chest was to do with too much beer last night and nothing to do with Ellie and her less-than-subtle rejection.

Laura was ready to leave by the time they got back, so Tom offered to take them home in his car. Ellie chattered happily in the back seat to him and Laura, enthusing about seeing Betsy again, but there was none of the personal warmth of yesterday evening. By the time he got back to his farm around mid-morning he was feeling grumpy and tired.

'I'm sure I can manage Dad on my own so we'll head home now, darling,' said his mum.

'OK,' he said shortly. He headed into the kitchen and poured a glass of water.

'Is everything all right?' asked Lynn, coming over and rubbing his shoulder, as she had when he was upset as a child.

'Of course, why wouldn't it be?'

'You seem out of sorts. Did you and Ellie have an argument?' she probed.

'No. What would we argue about?'

Now he was being as churlish as a teenager but he didn't know how to stop. Normally Mum brought out the best in him but today she seemed to be bringing out the worst — or maybe it was him. He needed a good night's rest and then he'd be back to normal.

'Ellie seemed very pale at breakfast and you're acting like a bear with a sore head since you got back from dropping her and Laura off. You were both fine when you went out last night, so . . . '

Tom shrugged. 'Ellie's being dramatic. She seems to think I'm about to force her to give up her career and make her live in Wales. Presumably as some sort of old-fashioned farmer's wife, but worse because I'll chain her to the kitchen sink and only allow her to wear long dresses with white pinafores over the top.'

Lynn laughed. 'Now who's being dramatic?'

Tom smiled and turned to his mum.

'It's a bit insulting, that's all. I'd never ask a girlfriend to give up her job.

Plus, and I think this is a really important point, I've only kissed her once and I've not asked her out on a date.'

'Perhaps you should.'

Tom snorted.

'I don't think so. It's not worth the hassle of going to fetch her whenever she runs a mile.'

'Nonsense,' said Lynn. 'It's worth all the effort you can make. You're as in love with her now as you were when you were both teenagers.'

15

For the next three days Ellie buckled down and prepared Gran's house for when she returned to London. She moved furniture around so it was easier to get past in a wheelchair. She chased social services and organised for a carer to come in three times a day.

She booked Gran's follow-up hospital appointments and arranged for a private physiotherapist to come to the house once a week after the cast was due to come off. She cooked lots of meals, following Gran's recipes to the letter, and filled the freezer with a variety of stews, cooked meats and puddings. She took Gran out to visit her friends and whenever there was a spare minute, she sat down with her and got out old family photographs. It was a joy to look at pictures of Grandad and to remember a time when they were all younger.

She managed to rewrite the first chapter of her thesis and this time she was pleased with what she'd written; finally she'd managed to convey her enthusiasm for the subject. She hoped her supervisor would be as pleased with her work.

Tom didn't contact her and she convinced herself she was glad.

It had been a mistake to kiss him after their trip to the pub. She could blame the wine but she hadn't had a drop since and she was still thinking about kissing him pretty much constantly. He was the most attractive man she'd spent time with in years, possibly ever. She'd behaved badly after the kiss, acting awkward and embarrassed and unsure as to what to say to him. He'd been charming and friendly and so kind when he'd taken her to see Betsy. He was a lot of fun, and she knew she would fall for him hard if she allowed herself.

But she didn't *want* to! As much as

she was enjoying life with Gran, she was still looking forward to getting back to work — and work was on the other side of the country. Starting a relationship would be a disaster. They'd only end up hurting each other in the long run.

She was chopping carrots to add to a bolognaise when her mobile rang. It was Tom. Her heart leaped, and she told it off sternly. There was to be no heart-leaping as far as Tom was concerned. She managed to wipe the carrot juice of her fingers and answer before he rang off.

'Hi, Tom,' she said cheerfully.

'Hey,' he said. 'Stuart's asked me to take Betsy for a walk this evening as he and his wife are going out. I was wondering whether you wanted to join me.'

'That sounds great — thanks.'

'We'll probably head to the beach because that's Betsy's favourite place.'

'Lovely,' said Ellie, who still hadn't had time to visit the beach since she'd arrived at Gran's over three weeks ago.

'I thought I'd take some food. Betsy's quite slow so we could eat while she explores the beach a bit.'

'Great,' said Ellie a little distractedly. The onions seemed to be cooking too quickly and smelled a little as if they were beginning to burn.

'I'll call round about six, then,' said Tom.

'Sure, see you later.'

She put the phone down and turned down the heat of the hob.

It was only later, when she was pulling on clean shorts just before Tom was due to arrive that she thought about the evening ahead. Tom's suggestion sounded suspiciously like a date.

The door bell rang before she could dwell on that thought for too long. Even so, she felt a bit jittery opening the front door.

Andrew and Tom were both standing outside in the early evening sun. Andrew greeted her politely and she mumbled something to him in response. She was far too busy looking at Tom. His half-smile was doing odd things to her stomach and she became fascinated by the way the sun caught the hairs in his pale stubble making the hair glint as he moved.

'Andrew,' shouted Laura from the lounge. 'Come on through.'

Ellie stood aside for Andrew to pass and then it was just her and Tom. The evening air was warm and he was wearing shorts and another of his faded T-shirts.

'Are you ready to go?' Tom asked briskly, obviously not as transfixed by her as she was with him. 'Only I won't come in with the two dogs.'

It said something about him and the way he looked that she hadn't noticed the two dogs at his feet.

'I'm ready,' she said, picking up her rucksack and pulling the front door closed behind her.

'Great. Do you want to take Betsy's lead and I'll take Tilly?' Tom handed over the lead. 'There's a shortcut to the beach through the fields so we can avoid the roads.'

'Are you allowed to walk through farmers' fields?' asked Ellie as they ducked under Gran's fence and out onto wide, open grassland.

Tilly tugged Tom forward but Betsy plodded sedately along and would not be hurried to keep up with the others.

'Some fields have access, others are private. These fields are private but as they belong to me, I'll let us off.' He grinned back at her. 'I've not got any cattle grazing on here today so it's OK. I'd use the roads with the dogs otherwise.'

Tilly was into every hedgerow, her tail whisking back and forth continuously as she dragged Tom along with her. Betsy maintained a steady pace, happy to stay by Ellie's legs.

'Do you own all this?' Ellie called out, gesturing to the land around them.

'We'll come to a lane in a minute and that'll be the end of my land. I own everything you can see that way,' he swept a hand behind them. The land disappeared over the brow of a large hill pretty quickly but Ellie was still impressed by the amount of outdoor space that was his.

'Who's looking after your cattle now?' Ellie asked. She'd not thought about it before coming to stay with Gran, but presumably Tom could never leave his cattle unsupervised. It must be a bind for a young man.

'I've two boys who work for me on a full-time contract. Sometimes they work into the evening so I can have the time off. It depends on the time of year and what I've got on.'

It was such an alien world to Ellie, who couldn't imagine what Tom's working day involved. What did being a farmer entail? But then, he probably couldn't imagine what her working day involved either.

'How's your dad?' she asked, even though she knew the answer. Gran was ringing Lynn for regular updates.

'He's hobbling around and driving Mum mad, which is pretty much the same as usual. He's cross with himself for not getting a good look at the perpetrator.'

'It's not his fault — we didn't see who it was either and we were in the same room as him.'

'True enough. Plus if Dad hadn't dramatically fallen on his face and caused a commotion, I might not have any livestock today. I can't thank him enough for that.'

They passed through a small gap in the hedgerow and cut into a narrow gravel lane.

'It's not far now,' said Tom.

'I know,' said Ellie as a host of memories flooded her. She remembered many sun-soaked afternoons wandering up the lane, her legs tired from clambering over rocks, her skin tight from dried seawater. A bucket often banging against her leg, full of interesting stones and shells she'd found at the beach. She'd once discovered an ammonite fossil and she still had it proudly displayed on her desk at home.

'Did you hide in this hedge and throw water bombs at me one summer?' she asked, remembering the irritation she'd felt at suddenly being soaked with water just after she'd dried off from an afternoon of swimming in the sea.

The tips of Tom's ears went pink. 'I was trying to get your attention. That was the year of the arrival of the big crush,' he confessed.

'Bringing Betsy for a walk is a much better idea for getting my attention,' she said, laughing.

'I'm more sophisticated than a thirteen-year-old boy. That's a relief!'

Ellie laughed again.

'Have you been to the beach much since you've been staying with Laura?' asked Tom in an abrupt change in conversation.

Ellie told him she'd not made it down once and the conversation flowed from there. By the time Ellie was spreading a blanket out for them to sit on, her jaw was aching from smiling so much.

The tide was on the way out leaving smooth, shiny sand in its wake. Betsy was content to pad around the soft, dry sand by Ellie's blanket while Tilly raced over to the emerging rock pools, sniffing them for hidden delights.

'Do you like Pimms?' asked Tom as he rummaged around inside a large green rucksack.

'I love it,' she said contentedly.

'Just as well, because I didn't think to bring anything else to drink.'

He started to pile picnic food onto the blanket.

'Wow. Is all this just for us?' Ellie asked as the food stacked up into a mini-mountain.

'I didn't know what you liked so I brought a little of everything,' he said.

Ellie tore off a large chunk of crispy baguette.

'I like the look of all of it,' she confirmed. 'I brought some cakes from The Café by the Sea. I'm slowly working my way through their entire menu. I'm getting addicted to the cook's baking; she's a genius.'

'Yeah, she's great,' said Tom, sounding distracted. Ellie felt a tinge of jealousy over the domestic goddess who lived so near Tom. Perhaps in years to come she'd hear news of their marriage. She shook her head — why was she thinking of this now?

Tom pulled out two plastic cups and poured them both generous measures of Pimms and lemonade from a flask. He handed one to Ellie who took it gratefully.

'Before we have this, there's something I want to say,' Tom said his voice suddenly serious.

Ellie felt a curl of something painful in the base of her stomach.

'Don't panic,' he said grinning. 'I'm not going to confess my undying love. I find you attractive and I think you like me too. You've got about two weeks left in Morwenna Bay; let's have some fun together while you're here with nothing serious on either side. And by fun I mean walks on the beach, a trip to Boxcomb's market, maybe dinner out, nothing sleazy.'

He winked at her and went back to fiddling with the picnic food, opening containers and peeling back lids. Ellie watched how the sunlight highlighted the blue of his eyes and didn't know what to say.

'You can say no,' said Tom. 'I won't be totally crushed — only a tiny bit.'

He held up a finger and thumb to show how little he'd mind and Ellie laughed.

'It sounds like a lovely idea,' she said. 'So long as we're both agreed it's nothing serious. I'm returning to London and long-distance relationships don't work. I've lots of experience of trying to maintain friendships from a distance with all the travelling I did as a child. It's painful and hard work and it would be a thousand times worse with a relationship.'

'It will be our holiday romance,' he

said, grinning, 'with not a water bomb in sight.'

She nodded and he leaned over and kissed her lightly.

'To us,' he said, tapping his plastic cup of Pimms against hers.

'To us,' she agreed, feeling as if she'd just agreed to something far scarier than turning up to give a lecture and realising your notes were still at home.

16

Tom paced back and forth in his lounge, straightening the already straight rug and brushing dust off the immaculate coffee table. Ellie was due to arrive in the next few minutes to begin their weekend of surveillance.

The last eight days had shot by as he'd spent as much time with her as possible, sorely neglecting the farm and making the lads work twice as hard as normal as they picked up his slack. Now Ellie was due to return to London on Wednesday, in only six days' time.

When he'd suggested a holiday fling to her he'd been hoping for one of two things to happen. Either she would fall desperately in love with him and be prepared to work at a long distance relationship until they came up with a better solution. Or, after spending more time with her, he'd decide that she wasn't all that wonderful and he wouldn't regret her leaving.

Neither of those scenarios had happened. His feelings had only become stronger and it felt a lot like he was in love with her. His mother certainly thought he was. He'd joked with Ellie about being broken-hearted when she left, but it seemed that was going to come true. Thinking of a life without her was making him feel nauseous.

She'd had fun with him; he knew that. She seemed to want to spend as much time with him as he did with her. But she didn't seem to be developing any irrevocable feelings. During their walk last night she'd told him she'd nearly finished the second chapter of her thesis and was on target for the meeting with her supervisor when she went back to work. She was so excited and passionate about the job — and she was looking forward to a future that didn't involve him.

He had the next two days to try and

change her mind about their future as a couple before he would have to admit defeat.

There was a tap on his back door and the sound of the soft click of it opening; she was here.

He took a deep breath. He was going to have to appear as relaxed and as happy as normal if he were to get through this weekend.

He made his way into the kitchen and found her putting some bags on the table.

'Hey,' he said bending to kiss her.

'Hey, yourself,' she said kissing him back. 'Did everything go to plan earlier?' she asked when they broke apart.

'Yep, we're completely alone. Apart from the pigs,' he amended.

Earlier, Tom had transported his cattle to Andrew's still-empty farm and locked them securely into his barn. Tom was paying his farmhands extra for two days so that they would stay with Andrew and help look after the cows.

The farm was eerily quiet without the animals and everyone who helped to look after them. Whatever happened, he would still have his cattle on Monday.

Even Tilly was staying at his parents' house. It had given him the peace of mind he needed this weekend. It was a long shot that someone would attack his farm anyway. Yes, he and Ellie had put it about that they'd be away this weekend but that didn't mean the thief would strike again.

Catching the thief had fallen to the back of his mind now that Ellie had arrived. All he could think about was having two days alone with her with no distractions.

'I managed to get hold two infrared cameras and three static surveillance cameras that we can put up outside and link to your computer. Where's the best place to set them up?' Ellie asked, placing a heavy-looking bag onto the table. She was obviously not on the same wavelength as him about their weekend alone. Romance didn't seem to be on her mind at all.

'Let's get two by the gate,' he said, reluctantly dragging his mind back to the job in hand. 'And one of them facing the door to my largest barn.'

'Where's your wireless router?' she asked, unpacking various bits of technology from her bag.

'In the study at the front of the house.'

'OK, that should be good enough for us to get an internet signal outside. Let's get started.'

After some wrangling they managed to secure two cameras to trees just outside the farm gates and one on the corner of the house. The ones in the trees were nicely hidden by the abundant green foliage but the one on the house was a bit more obvious.

'We'll just have to hope it doesn't stand out too much in the dark,' said Ellie, frowning slightly.

'Hopefully they won't get as far as the barn,' said Tom. 'The chains on the front gate are thick. I hope that's enough to put them off.'

'Hmm,' said Ellie. 'It's certainly a better defence than the locks at Andrew's and Roger's farms but it's not impenetrable.'

'Let's hope we get close enough to get some good photographs, then.'

'Yes, let's,' said Ellie. 'Let's go and hook the cameras up to your computer.'

*   *   *

After another frustrating half an hour where it seemed that the system wouldn't work at all they managed to get images feeding from all three cameras and displaying on the computer monitor.

'Now what?' asked Ellie as they stepped back to admire their handiwork.

'Dinner,' Tom suggested. 'I've made a curry. It's one of the few dishes I do well.'

'Great, I'm starving,' she said, skipping away from him and into the kitchen.

'Something smells amazing,' she said as she started to lift lids off pans and peer into them.

'If you grab some plates, I'll dish up,' he said, trying to catch his breath. She was beautiful, moving about his kitchen as if she belonged there. He didn't know what he was going to do when she was gone in a few days' time.

He'd been trying to show off, and earlier he'd made the dough for his own naan bread. He rolled out two large portions and put them in the oven. While he was waiting for them to cook he filled two plates with spicy dhansak and pungent lentils with Thai fragrant rice.

'I'd suggest a glass of wine,' he said, 'but I suspect drinking while on a surveillance operation is a no-go.'

She laughed and said, 'A glass of wine might send me to sleep so it's probably best I avoid it. Another time, perhaps.'

He nodded but they both knew there wasn't going to be another time. With her leaving in a few days, they probably wouldn't have another uninterrupted evening together after this weekend. He didn't want to bring the mood down by pointing it out.

They sat in one corner of his dining table, their legs touching. He dimmed the lights and they spoke quietly, talking about everything and nothing at all. He tried to make her laugh and for the most part he managed it pretty well, but his mind kept flicking to the thought that he wanted her at the table with him for always.

By early evening they had fallen quiet.

'It's unlikely he'll strike before it gets dark,' said Ellie.

'We'll both probably feel more comfortable if we sat in the study. That way we can keep an eye on the camera feed and an ear out for any vehicles heading this way,' Tom suggested.

His study had a brown leather couch along one wall. It was worn and soft, and great for sinking into with a girl in his arms. Tom put the TV on quietly and they watched a film with the sound turned down low. When the credits rolled Tom couldn't remember a single thing that had happened for the last two hours.

Ellie was getting heavy in his arms.

'Shall I get a sleeping bag?' he asked. 'You could get a few hours' sleep and then we'll swap over.'

She nodded gratefully and seconds after she'd slid into the covers she was asleep. He alternated between watching her breathing and staring at the images showing on the monitor. Hours passed and nothing happened. He found he was watching Ellie far more than the monitor. When he couldn't keep his eyes open any longer he gently woke Ellie.

'Hey,' he whispered.

She stretched and scrunched her eyes even tighter. He grinned and brushed his lips over her forehead.

'I hate to wake you,' he said quietly. 'But I just can't keep my eyes open a second longer.'

She opened her eyes and stared at him in confusion for a moment. Then she glanced at her watch.

'You should have woken me much sooner,' she said. 'You've been awake most of the night.'

He shrugged. 'It is my farm we're defending. I figure it's me who should bear the brunt of the hard work.'

'Don't be silly,' she said as she struggled out of the sleeping bag. 'I'm here to help you. Please get some rest while I take watch.'

He gratefully climbed into the covers still warm from her body and the world turned black before he'd even laid his head down.

He woke hours later feeling as if he'd lain on a hard board for days. The sofa was only comfortable for sitting on, it turned out.

Ellie was standing next to the settee holding two mugs of coffee.

'Here,' she said holding out one of the mugs towards him. 'This should make you feel better.'

'Thanks,' he murmured as he took the mug from her. He wrapped his fingers around the cup and sighed. 'The whole night was a waste of time, then.'

'There's always tonight.'

He pulled himself into a sitting position and she came and sat next to him. He laced their fingers and they sat in silence for a while watching nothing happen on the computer monitor.

'I was so sure . . . ' she said.

'There's always tonight,' he agreed, 'and if nothing happens, well at least I've got some surveillance cameras out of it.'

She huffed in amusement and snuggled closer.

'I should phone Gran. She'll want to update her incident room with the latest news or lack of.'

'Actually,' said Tom his arm tightening around her shoulder. 'I can think of a better way to spend our time.'

'Oh, really?' she said, her beautiful smile breaking across her face.

'Yeah,' he said and lowered his mouth to hers.

It turned out the couch was fairly comfortable after all.

17

Ellie lay on her back and stared at a tiny crack in the corner of the ceiling. For the last ten minutes she and Tom had been playing the 'If we were really at the festival . . . ' game. It was her go.

'If we were really at the festival we'd be eating pulled pork burgers in brioche rolls with a generous side helping of curly fries.'

'Why do all your festival-related wishes contain food or drink?' asked Tom, lying next to her on the floor of the study, his fingers laced with hers.

'I'm hungry.'

'I'll go get us some food,' said Tom but he didn't move. Like her he was feeling sloth-like with the lack of fresh air. He'd suggested they stand out in the back garden for a moment but she'd vetoed that idea. If anyone was watching the house and saw them standing there, then the whole effort of the weekend would be wasted. They were caged inside until Sunday evening. It was a weird feeling.

'If we were really at the festival we'd be drinking Pimms and lemonade in glasses filled with strawberries, cucumber and mint,' said Ellie wistfully.

Tom laughed. 'OK, OK, I get the hint. What would you like to eat?'

'I really want a bacon sandwich,' said Ellie, pulling a face.

'What's the strange face for?' asked Tom.

'I feel really bad about this, but I've been craving bacon since we heard the pigs snuffling about earlier,' she confessed.

He laughed and pulled himself up.

'OK, you stay here and watch nothing happening on the monitor. I'll go and get two guilt-laden bacon baguettes. Are you a tomato or a brown sauce girl?'

'Brown sauce, please,' she confirmed. When she heard the reassuring noise of bacon frying in a pan she pulled herself up and climbed onto the leather sofa to get a better view of the monitor. Night was falling again and she had everything crossed that tonight would be the night they solved the mystery. Otherwise she'd return to London having let Tom and her gran down and she didn't want that on her conscience. Not when they'd become such good friends.

She blushed a little. OK — not since when she and Tom had become such good lovers.

It was strange to think that in less than five days she'd be on her way back to London and that she probably wouldn't see him again for a long time — if ever.

Yesterday Gran had dropped a bombshell on Ellie that she still hadn't had the heart to tell Tom. It felt too much like an end to an era and she didn't want to bring things to an end just yet. She still had five days left to go.

Before Ellie had come over to Tom's

house, Gran had asked her to join her in the lounge. Ellie was expecting an inquisition on what was happening between her and Tom but Gran had blindsided her by gently explaining that she had decided to sell her home. Ellie couldn't imagine Gran living anywhere but in the whitewashed cottage that had been her home for fifty years.

'I'm going to live with Andrew,' Gran had said, shocking Ellie, who hadn't seen that decision coming. She'd imagined that Gran and Andrew were more friends who kept each other company rather than anything else. The knowledge that the relationship was more serious than she'd imagined had come as a bit of a body blow — a reaction she'd tried very hard to hide from Gran.

'The insurance company are still being difficult,' Gran had continued, 'and I want to help him. I'll sell my home and with the profit I'll invest in his farm. It's a business deal with benefits.'

She'd smiled at Ellie and stroked her hair back from her face lovingly.

'But what if the insurance company come through and pay what they owe?' Ellie had asked, clutching at straws.

'It doesn't matter. I've made my decision. There's no point me living in this great big house all on my own, love. And no, that isn't me trying to make you feel guilty and force you into moving here to be with me. It's me being practical. Andrew and I have agreed that I will have an area of the house to myself. I'm used to my own ways but now I'll have company as well.'

Ellie had agreed that it sounded like a good, practical idea. Then she'd gone upstairs to get her bags ready for her stay with Tom and she'd shed a few tears. It had felt a little like losing Grandad all over again, but she knew Gran had to move on with her life and she didn't begrudge her newfound love.

Ellie had promised Gran she would visit more often and she had made her promise to visit her in return, but with Gran no longer living so near Tom, their paths never need cross again. At the beginning of their affair she'd wanted it to end with a clean break, but now the thought of not seeing him again was making her feel bleak. There was no alternative, though. She had her life in London; he had his life here.

Her eyes, which had wandered while she mused on Gran moving house, caught a movement on one of the cameras. She looked again, closer this time.

'Tom,' she hissed.

The sounds of cooking continued in the kitchen.

'Tom,' she hissed louder.

'Yes,' he called back.

'I think something's happening.'

She heard the sound of a pan being dragged across a hob and then footsteps as he ran into the study. Together they watched as a man, dressed all in black, stood where Tom's gate met the wall. The figure was as deep into the shadows as the wall would allow. He was very still with his hands thrust into his jacket pockets. It was difficult to tell with the lack of light but it appeared as if the figure was looking towards the house.

Five minutes passed and he didn't move; neither did Tom or Ellie.

Then the figure turned slowly away from the gate and disappeared up the hill away from the village below.

Ellie and Tom let out identical long breaths.

'Can you zoom in on that picture?' said Tom indicating towards the best image they had on the monitor.

'We can but I'm not sure that we'll get anything helpful from a bigger image. The man was wearing a hoodie and a cap pulled down low. I doubt we'll be able to make out any detail on his face.'

'What good's the camera, then?' asked Tom, frustrated.

'It's good but it doesn't come equipped with X-ray vision,' said Ellie, equally disappointed.

She pulled the keyboard towards her and fiddled with the settings. The picture of the man filled the screen but as Ellie had predicted, it was impossible to make out any features on his shadowed face.

'Even if we could see who it was, without a transporter or anything else incriminating, it's just a picture of a man out for a walk. One who's acting suspiciously, admittedly — but not one who's doing anything wrong,' said Ellie.

They sat in silence for a moment, looking at the image, trying to get any detail they could glean but it was worse than when they'd been in the warehouse. In this it was impossible to confirm that it was even a man standing there, although the width of the shoulders suggested that it was.

'I'll go and finish the sandwiches,' said Tom despondently.

'OK.'

Tom trudged back to the kitchen and

Ellie heard the hiss of the gas starting up again.

'Tom,' she called out sharply, 'I think you'd better come back.'

She heard the pan being dragged again and the thud of Tom's footsteps returning to the study.

'What is it?' he demanded.

'Can you hear that?' she asked.

In the distance they could hear the rumbling of a large vehicle coming towards them.

'This could be it,' she said, her hands shaking slightly.

The noise got nearer.

'Yeah,' he said, 'this is it.'

'Right,' she said, handing him a camera. 'We've got to get a picture of them in the act. We'll do as we agreed earlier. I'll go and hide by the gate, you hide opposite the barn. We don't engage with them under any circumstances. OK?'

'OK,' answered Tom.

Ellie bent over to pull on her black trainers but Tom grabbed her arm, stopping her.

'Ellie,' he said urgently. 'Don't do anything risky. Please don't put yourself in harm's way. I couldn't bear it.'

'I won't,' she said rising up on tiptoes to kiss him. 'You must promise me the same.'

'I promise,' he said reluctantly.

Together they made their way to the back of his house. Silently he opened the back door and slid out into the night. She followed. He looked at her intently and then nodded. They would go their separate ways and meet back at the house when it was all over.

★   ★   ★

Ellie crept round the side of the house, keeping as close as she could to disguise her movements. She made it to the outer wall just as a large truck thundered down the road and pulled to a stop outside the farm entrance. She could make out the shape of two people in the front cabin but there were no lights anywhere and it was impossible to make out who they were. She tutted in annoyance.

The driver hopped out of the cabin and made his way to the gate, carrying bolt cutters. Although she couldn't make out any features, she raised the camera and took a few shots. The man reached across to cut the thick chain and Ellie froze.

It couldn't be. Surely not! She squinted, unable to believe what she was seeing, but before she could take a photograph the man dropped his arm and pulled the remains of the chain through the gate. Throwing the chain to one side, he pushed the gate open and the transporter pulled into Tom's courtyard.

Ellie, acting on autopilot, took more photos as the men set to work. They were a well-oiled team and they didn't speak. From her vantage point by the gate she heard a grunt of surprise when the barn was opened and found to be empty. The driver efficiently cut open the bolts on the remaining sheds but after finding the third one empty of cattle he made a gesture to his partner and they both jumped back into the truck.

Within seconds they were pulling out of the courtyard and heading back away from the farm. Ellie lost sight of them quickly.

Instead of returning to the house as they'd agreed, she ran over to Tom's hiding place.

She found Tom picking up the ruined bolts and swearing viciously. She stood back for a moment and waited until he'd vented his anger.

'Sorry, Ellie,' he said, finally realising she was standing behind him. 'I'm just so frustrated that two men could casually walk onto my land and try to take everything I've worked for away from me. Instead of punching them as I should have done, I just stood there and took their photograph. I think my hands were shaking too badly for me to get a decent shot. Please tell me you have some tangible evidence.'

'Let's go back inside,' said Ellie gently, 'and call the police. They need to make a note of what happened here tonight. Even though nothing was taken, damage has been done to your property.'

Tom nodded. 'But did you get any good pictures?' he asked again.

'Let's take a look inside,' she said firmly.

Once inside, Ellie made them both a sweet cup of tea and then she phoned the police. They came out almost instantly and Tom and Ellie showed them the photographs and recordings from the surveillance cameras. Despite his worries, Tom had managed to get several decent shots of the men. Their faces were concealed but it would be possible to work out their height and build from the images. The surveillance cameras had done their job and had captured the whole of the attack. If the two men were caught, it would be damning evidence against them. The police were a little cross at the risks

Ellie and Tom had taken, but they took the evidence away and promised to be in touch.

★ ★ ★

The visit by the police had lasted hours, and it was early morning before Ellie and Tom were alone again, but neither of them were in the mood for sleep. Ellie helped him patch up some splintered panels on the barns. Working only in the soft dawn-light it wasn't easy to see what they were doing, but it felt proactive to be moving so they carried on. They only spoke to direct each other's movements and for almost an hour they barely spoke a word.

'What I can't get over,' said Tom eventually, 'is how *easy* it was for them. They cut through my thick chains like butter. I feel like I've been violated.' He laughed humourlessly. 'That sounds a bit dramatic, seeing how nothing was taken.'

'I would imagine feeling violated is

quite a common feeling for someone who's had the experience you've just been through. You're justified in feeling upset.'

Tom nodded and rubbed his eyes.

'What really angers me,' he said, 'is that we didn't catch them. They're free to make someone else feel like this or potentially ruin some poor famer's life like they did with Roger and Andrew. They were right in front of me. Why didn't I just grab them?'

He kicked a plank of wood and then rubbed his toe, muttering words of pain. Ellie couldn't bear to see him like this.

'I saw something,' she confessed.

'What did you see?' Tom asked sharply.

'Something potentially damning,' she said sadly. 'I need to double-check what I've seen before I can make any accusations.'

'What was it and why didn't you tell the police?'

'I need more time,' said Ellie distantly.

'Why?'

'Because if I'm right about what I saw, then I think I know who it is and you won't like it. Neither will Gran.'

18

Ellie had never seen Gran's dining room so full. Andrew was seated next to Gran, his arm resting along the back of her wheelchair. Roger and Mary were sipping tea and making small talk with Tom's parents, who kept surreptitiously glancing at their son whenever they thought he wasn't looking.

Tom was sitting on a dining chair pushed back from the table. His arms were resting on his knees and he was studying his hands intently. Even Tilly seemed to have picked up on his mood. She'd only managed a few wags of her tail when she'd entered the house earlier and she was now slumped despondently at Tom's feet.

Ellie hadn't seen Tom since the night of the botched attempt to steal cattle from his farm and tomorrow she was returning to London. He'd wanted to see her but she'd made excuses to avoid him, even though it hurt her to do so. He would have put pressure on her to reveal what she knew and she hadn't been prepared to make accusations until she was a hundred per cent positive that she was right. Time had run out for them as a couple. It was what she wanted — so it shouldn't feel as though a dark hole was opening up in front of her, but it did.

She cleared her throat. Everyone turned to look at her expectantly.

'Thank you all for coming,' she said nervously. 'I've been working really hard over the last couple of days to tie up some loose ends on this case. I wanted to be sure before I told all of you my findings. I believe what I'm about to tell you is correct but once I've told you, I want to leave it with you all to decide how to proceed from here.'

Everyone nodded and stayed silent, waiting.

Ellie turned round her gran's white-board so that it was facing the rest of the room.

'I hope you don't mind but I want to give everyone an overview of the case and everything that's led me to this point. I want you to understand where I'm coming from with my conclusion,' she began.

The occupants of the room nodded.

'After the first robbery we were made aware of, it made sense to consider you, Andrew, as the prime suspect. You stood to gain the most money if you got away with the crime.'

Gran's pale face turned pink but Andrew rubbed her arm reassuringly.

'It makes sense,' he said. 'It's what the insurance company have been claiming since the beginning of all this. I understand they thought I could get the insurance money, sell up the farm and make a tidy profit. Now that there have been similar attacks they are coming round to the idea that I'm not involved, but I could have been planning to use all that money to move to the Costa del Sol.'

'Exactly,' said Ellie, glad he wasn't taking the news he'd been her first suspect badly.

'Then there was the attack on Roger's farm,' she continued. 'If we were considering Andrew we had to consider Roger too, even though instinct was telling me neither of you were guilty.'

'Costa del Sol is going to be busy with Welsh famers,' joked Roger.

Everyone laughed apart from Tom, who managed a weak smile. Lynn frowned at her son, obviously concerned by his lack of reaction. Ellie was finding it unnerving to see him without his customary grin. She knew that she was partly responsible for his mood and that by the end of the evening she was going to make him feel much worse. Her stomach tightened and she swallowed. She needed to get on with this.

'Tom and I ruled you both out when

we went to the warehouses in Box-comb. All the evidence points to your animals having been kept there for a short period and I'm sorry to tell you that the conditions inside the ware-house aren't good.'

Both Andrew and Roger looked pained.

'If it helps, we don't think they were kept there for more than a day or two,' Ellie added.

'Not really, dear,' said Andrew. Roger shook his head in agreement. Ellie glanced at Mary; tears were running down her face. This was awful.

Ellie nodded, not sure what to say next.

'That's why I was able to confirm to Ellie that you two definitely couldn't be involved,' said Tom. 'I knew you would never keep animals in those conditions.'

'Yes,' said Ellie, grateful for his contribution. 'That was our first posi-tive proof although probably not a point that would stand up in court. However, later that day we caught sight of the real thief and although we couldn't make out any features, the way he moved and his build ruled both of you out.'

'He was a young man, you mean,' said Roger, his eyes lit up with mischief.

Ellie laughed. 'We couldn't tell what age he was because it was dark, but we could see enough to know it wasn't either of you two.'

'That was tactful,' said Andrew, smiling.

She took one of the marker pens and crossed Roger's and Andrew's names off the whiteboard.

'This brings us to suspect number two. Simon Hawley.' She tapped his name on the board and Roger and Mary shuffled in their seats. The others looked up, alert now that they thought they were getting somewhere. It seemed the whole group was expecting his guilt.

'He's a real menace,' said Roger angrily. 'I should never have allowed him on my farm when he was younger.

I was a trusting fool.'

'He does seem to have had a colourful history,' said Ellie. 'I've spent the last few days looking into him and he seems to crop up in over half the crimes recorded locally over the last ten years.'

'I hope he rots in prison,' said Roger, uncharacteristically vehement.

'Tom and I had the luck to come across him while we were in Boxcomb and we heard him making plans to meet up with someone called Pete later that day. I'll come to Peter in a moment,' she said tapping Peter's name on the whiteboard, 'but let's stay with Simon a moment.'

'Do we have to?' asked Roger.

'Shush,' murmured Mary. 'Let's hear what Ellie has to say.'

'Simon looked the most likely suspect. He had a previous history of stealing cattle and is a known criminal — but unfortunately for us, it's not him.'

Roger gasped and everyone sat up

straighter, even Tom. She'd shocked them all.

'How do you know for sure?' asked Roger.

'I found out that he has an alibi for at least three of the raids.'

'He faked them all,' claimed Roger.

'I'm sorry, Roger, but it's almost impossible. During the attack on your farm, he was at his daughter's wedding in Greece. When Tom and I saw him in Boxcomb he was on his way to meet his friend Pete Robinson for an evening at the races. I spoke to the police yesterday and there is footage of him at the course. He didn't leave until gone midnight. It's not enough time for him to get to Tom's farm only an hour later. For the final attack last Saturday night he was in police custody for a different crime. He has three cast iron alibis. He's not guilty.'

'Well I'm blessed,' said Roger, sitting back in his chair. 'I was so sure.'

There was a general nodding of heads around the room as everyone took in the news.

'Next we come to Peter,' continued Ellie. 'Gran first became suspicious of him because he and Charlotte seemed to suddenly become very wealthy and we couldn't tell where all the money was coming from. He has worked on all your farms so has experience with different types of livestock and he's very strong, so he could easily cope with the physical aspects involved in a crime like the ones we're looking at. Like all of you I really didn't want it to be Peter. Not only because he seems like a decent guy, his fiancée is lovely and I didn't want to destroy her happiness.'

Lynn covered her mouth with her hands.

'Please tell me it's not Peter,' she murmured. 'I used to teach him in Sunday School when he was a little boy. He was such a sweetheart and he's so polite even now. Whenever he sees me he asks how we're all doing. I really, really don't want it to be him.'

Ellie put her pen down briefly.

'I can stop now,' she said. 'I have to warn you that no one is going to be happy with the outcome of the investigation.'

Silence reigned.

'Go on, love,' said Gran eventually. 'We have to know. The attacks have got to stop.'

She looked around the room. Everyone, even Lynn, nodded back at her.

'I did something I'm not particularly proud to have done,' confessed Ellie. 'On Monday I called round to Charlotte's house and invited myself in. I was quite pushy and made her give me a tour of her house. She was a bit bemused but luckily she is a lovely person and didn't seem to mind. Has anyone ever been in her house?'

Everyone shook her head.

'I didn't think so. Her house is very pretty. She's a good eye for decoration and they've created a lovely home. Nothing in there seems particularly pricey but there were a lot of wedding brochures lying everywhere. We spent a good hour or more looking through them and I can safely say that she wants their wedding to be spectacular — and by that I mean it's going to cost a fortune.'

'He never could resist giving Charlotte whatever she wanted,' said Lynn. 'It's a strong motive to get more money by any means possible.'

Andrew nodded, 'There's no way he could afford an expensive wedding on the amount he earns from a farmhand.'

'That's what I thought,' said Ellie pointing her pen at Andrew. 'And when I'd seen the plans for the ice sculpture she's planning I was almost certain that Peter had to be involved. But did you know, and I suspect from this conversation that none of you do, that Peter is an exceptionally talented artist?'

There were gasps of surprise around the room and Ellie smiled. This was a good surprise, so different from the surprise that was coming up.

'Charlotte took me out to a massive shed they have in their back garden,' she continued. 'Inside is his studio. It's — well, words failed me when I stepped inside, his paintings are exquisite. He has an online shop, which Charlotte manages when she's not at work at the Post Office, and they sell everything from there. The local community don't know about it because he's very modest. He'd have kept his painting as a private hobby if Charlotte hadn't insisted that he find a gallery to display his work. From this he's had commissions from around the world.

'He doesn't need to do any of the physical labouring he does but he likes to burn off his energy to clear his mind before he starts painting. If you get a chance to visit his studio then I highly recommend it.'

'Well, well,' said Andrew leaning back in his chair. 'Who would have thought young Peter would have such a hidden talent.'

'I bought a painting he's done of the bay,' said Ellie, fishing out a small canvas from a carrier bag at her feet and holding it up. As soon as she'd seen it she knew she had to have it. The painting was of Morwenna Bay with a tide that had just turned and was heading out. She felt that if she could step into it she would feel the soft, wet sand on her feet and the sound of waves crashing against the shore. Ellie passed it to Gran.

'It's beautiful,' said Gran, holding it up. Andrew leaned over her shoulder to get a better look.

'It cost me an arm and a leg, so don't damage it,' said Ellie with a smile.

'Didn't Charlotte give you a discount?' asked Gran, passing the painting on to Lynn.

'She did, but even at half price it was still more than I would normally pay for a painting.'

'This doesn't mean he's innocent, though,' pointed out Tom. 'It just means it's less likely to be him.'

'That's true,' said Ellie. 'Without being too obvious about it, at least I hope I wasn't, I asked what they'd been up to at the weekend. Charlotte showed me photographs of them at a gallery event to celebrate Peter's latest collection. I Googled the gallery when I got back to Gran's after visiting Charlotte and it confirms that there was a party for Peter and his work on Saturday evening. There are photographs on the site with Peter and Charlotte posing next to his paintings. Charlotte tells me the party went on until late in the evening and the gallery is in Boxcomb. I rang the hotel she claims they stayed at they have a record of the couple checking out on Sunday morning. He also doesn't have time to get from drinking wine in Boxcomb to your farm and back in the time frame available.'

'Everyone on the board is innocent, then,' observed Gran.

'Everyone that is, apart from *this* person.' Ellie pointed to the question mark.

'That's not a person,' returned Gran.

'It represents someone we hadn't thought about and whom we didn't suspect,' said Ellie.

The room went silent. Shoulders tensed; she had everyone's attention.

'Before I tell you who it is I want to tell you my reasoning behind my accusation.'

'Can you not just tell us who it is?' asked Roger. 'Get this dreadful suspense over with.'

'I could, but I don't think you'll believe me without hearing my rationale.'

'OK,' said Roger. 'Let's hear it.'

'When Gran first asked me to investigate the case she wanted to look at the means, motive and opportunity for each person. The motive for this person is money. They need it and they need it desperately. Without it they will lose everything. As I explained to Gran, means stands for the ability for the suspect to commit the crime. This person has spent all their life around farmland. They understand how it works and they have the right contacts. As for opportunity, well, that is harder to prove, but this person knows the ins and outs of all the people in this room.'

Tom groaned and put his head in his hands; he'd worked it out and he clearly didn't like what he'd concluded. Everyone else still looked puzzled.

'I wouldn't have thought of this person if I hadn't been at Tom's house taking photographs. When the perpetrator reached up to cut the chain on Tom's gate, his jacket sleeve rode up and I saw a small part of a very distinctive tattoo on his arm. The same tattoo I saw on him when he was handing me a glass of juice at The Ship.'

'It's Mike,' said Tom incredulously. 'I can't believe it! We've been friends for twenty years. How could he even think about doing this to me?'

Everyone stared at Tom.

Lynn shook her head. 'It can't be Mike. He's one of our family's closest friends.'

Ellie glanced at Gran. She was dabbing her eyes with a handkerchief.

'I'm sorry,' said Ellie sadly. 'It is him. I have absolutely no doubt.'

Tom stood up abruptly and left the room.

19

Tom stood in Laura's garden and looked towards his own fields. His cattle were grazing, moving lazily over the grassland. Everything looked normal — but today had turned into a nightmare.

Mike, one of his oldest friends, was responsible for delivering a series of crushing blows to the community. It was going to be so hard for everyone in the village to accept — and yet there was no way he couldn't go to the police with the information. Tom couldn't allow Mike to go on committing crimes just because of their shared history and because he liked the man.

Tom closed his eyes as he thought of Mike's parents, their gentle smiles and their supportive actions. They were going to be devastated. The fallout from this revelation was going to be huge.

He heard light footsteps approaching.

He didn't need to turn round to know it was Ellie. She slipped her arm through his and he turned and pulled her into his arms.

'I should have worked it out,' he said gruffly.

'No one wants to think a friend is guilty. I hardly know him and I don't want him to be guilty either, he's been lovely to me while I've been here.'

'It's obvious when you think about it. He and I worked on the farm for Dad when we were younger so he'd know how to handle animals. He would also know all our movements because we talk about them freely at the pub.'

Ellie nodded against his chest.

'He told me,' she said, 'not long after I came to stay, that the brewery had put up the rent for the pub. After I saw his tattoo during the raid at your house I contacted someone I know on the police force and she found out for me that he is still in a huge amount of debt after all the renovations he's had done.

He's missed a couple of mortgage payments and he's in danger of being repossessed. He's in a desperate situation and reacted desperately. It's not a personal attack.'

'It doesn't matter if he hasn't intended to hurt us. It still feels as if he has. I don't know how we all go forward from here,' Tom said desperately.

'Roger and Andrew have said that they will go to the police. You don't need to be involved.'

'I do,' he said.

He rested his forehead against hers.

'I guess this is goodbye for us,' he said quietly.

She nodded.

'I hope you don't mind,' he said, 'but I won't come to the bus station to see you off. It would be too hard.'

She nodded again; tears were falling down her face. He wiped them away with his thumb.

'These weeks have been a blast, Ellie. I won't regret our time together. I wish we'd had longer.'

He kissed her. Her hands curled into his T-shirt.

'Are you sure about ending this between us?' he said roughly after they'd broken apart. 'Are you absolutely sure? Because us ending this relationship feels like a terrible mistake to me.'

Ellie said, her voice croaky, 'Long distance relationships don't work, Tom.'

'OK,' he said. He untangled her fists from his T-shirt and kissed her hands. 'Goodbye, Ellie.'

He took a step back and looked down at her. He tried to smile, hoping his face didn't show how sick he felt. He raised his hand to stroke her cheek but thought better of it. He was going to have to walk away before made a fool of himself and fell to his knees to beg her to stay.

He turned and took a few steps towards the fence that separated Laura's property from his. He walked slowly, hoping Ellie would call him back, but she didn't.

He climbed over Laura's low fence and onto his own land and walked away.

20

Ellie curled upon her bed in her Gran's house. Her case was packed and placed by the bedroom door ready to go early tomorrow morning.

She'd forced a goodbye meal down and had rebuffed Gran anytime she brought up the subject of Tom. Gran also thought she was making a terrible mistake ending their brief relationship.

'It's a holiday romance, Gran,' Ellie had argued. 'Those don't last in the real world.'

'I don't understand why you're not even willing to try. He's such a lovely man. You won't meet another one like him.'

Ellie had sighed and taken a large gulp of wine.

'I know long distance relationships don't work because I've moved so many times. How many friends have I kept in touch with from all those different countries I lived in as a child? None. And it hurts when you like someone so much but they don't respond to your letters. It shows they didn't care as much about you as you did about them. I don't want to go through that again, especially when the feelings would be stronger this time. Eventually one of us would lose interest in the effort of staying together. It would be a long, drawn-out, painful goodbye instead of a clean break.'

'It would be different with Tom,' Gran argued.

'I don't see how you can know that,' said Ellie, huffing out a laugh despite her heart breaking. 'Please, let's talk about something else.'

Fortunately Gran had taken the hint and they had discussed Gran's plans for Andrew's farmhouse. Ellie hoped Andrew knew what he was getting himself into. Gran's ideas for extending the farmhouse to provide extensive ground floor accommodation sounded worthy of a *Grand Designs* episode.

After Ellie had finally swallowed the last mouthful of cheesecake, she'd been able to convince Gran she'd eaten enough and she was allowed into the kitchen to wash up.

Away from Gran's concerned eyes, she'd flipped on the radio and allowed herself to cry, hoping that the music and running water would drown out the sound. She'd managed to get herself under control by the time she was putting the last plate in the cupboard, and she held herself together through the normal night-time routine, but as soon as she was on her own in her bedroom she started to cry again.

Midnight had passed and every time she thought she'd got herself under control, the crying started up again. She'd never felt like this. Several boyfriends had come and gone and she'd not shed a single tear, or even felt mild regret. The ending of previous relationships had been a relief — but this felt as if a black chasm was opening up in front of her from which there was no escape.

Her pillow was soggy. She turned it over, only to find she'd already done that once before, so now both sides were wet with her tears. She let out a shuddering sigh; she was a mess.

She loved Tom; she'd admitted that to herself several hours ago, but the realisation hadn't made her feel any better.

No matter how she felt about him, she wasn't going to go back on her word. She'd had her career path mapped out since she was just a teenager. In comparison she'd hardly wanted Tom for any time at all. She'd begrudge him if she didn't follow her dream, and starting a relationship with resentment in her heart was a recipe for disaster.

She rolled over to the other side of the bed. It was time to get the other pillow wet.

A light tapping sounded at her window.

She raised her head. Had she imagined it?

The tapping became more insistent. It sounded as if someone outside wanted her attention. But who could it be?

She glanced at the clock. It was nearly one in the morning.

She flung back the cover and slipped her feet into her flip flops. She tiptoed over to the window.

This time there was no mistaking the noise.

She lifted up the edge of the curtain and peered round through the tiny gap.

Tom was looking back at her; the smile was back in his eyes. He looked like his normal self, which was a bit of a dent to her pride. She'd been crying her heart out over him and he'd recovered within a few hours of them parting for good.

She pulled the curtains back properly and unlatched the window, swinging it in towards her.

'What are you doing?' she asked.

'Trying to get your attention,' he said. 'Are you OK? You look a bit . . .' He wrinkled his nose as he gazed at her. She brushed her hair back from her face self-consciously. She wished she'd looked in the mirror before opening the window.

'I'm fine,' she said defiantly.

He raised an eyebrow.

'I may have been crying a little bit,' she conceded with a slight smile.

He leaned on the windowsill and cupped her face in his hand. His thumb delicately stroked her chin. She smiled sadly.

'I thought we'd said goodbye,' she whispered.

'Yeah,' said Tom, 'but after I left you, I did some thinking.'

'About Mike?' she asked. 'Because I am sure he's guilty.'

'I believe you,' he said briskly. 'And although I have thought about what Mike's been up to over the last few months a lot, it's not why I'm here.'

'Oh?'

'Your objection to us being together is that we live on opposite sides of the country, is that right? It's not that you think I'm a hideous troll and this is your polite way of trying to get out of a relationship with me?'

She laughed. 'I love you,' she said honestly.

'Good, because I love you too,' he said, a grin lighting up his eyes.

Her heart squeezed and she reached up to touch his hand, which was now resting lightly on her shoulder.

'Do you want to come in?' she asked.

'Yes.' He lifted a foot up to the window sill.

'You could come in through the front door,' she said, laughing.

'This is more romantic,' he said, grinning as he slid clumsily through the window and landed in a heap on her bedroom floor.

She snorted and helped him up. He tugged her over to the bed and they sat next to each other on the edge, holding hands tightly.

'Tom,' she said urgently. 'All my relationships with friends and relatives have been long distance and they never work out properly. I mean, I hardly see my own parents. We don't have the same relationship you have with your parents who you see all the time. I do love you, but I can't put us through the trauma of living so far apart.'

'You're very dramatic,' he commented gently. He drew his phone out of his pocket. 'I've been doing some research and I've got two suggestions.'

He disentangled their fingers and started scrolling through the screens.

'I know you've always dreamed of being a criminologist, but you've said you enjoy the practical side of your research and you've really enjoyed playing detective these last few weeks. My first suggestion — and I admit it's a bit out there — is that you think about setting up as a private investigator. If you like the idea, I've had a load of ideas on how we could make it work.'

She nodded slowly. It was a crazy

suggestion but it wasn't totally ridiculous. It was something she'd considered herself.

'Or,' he said dropping the phone slightly and clicking onto an internet page. He held it out to her. 'If that doesn't interest you, there are hundreds of farms for sale in the South East. I could sell mine and move to be nearer to you. I'm sure we could find somewhere commutable for you, but with enough land for me.'

She didn't say anything as she scrolled through the tiny pictures of farms for sale.

'You'd do that for me?' she asked, her voice tremulous. 'What about your family and your roots here? I can't ask you to give up all of that.'

'You're not asking me, I'm volunteering. I love living here, but I'm not so devoted to the place that I can't adapt. Home is where you are from now on.'

She gave him back his phone and he placed it on the bed behind them. Her heart was racing. No one had ever made her feel so special or so wanted.

'You don't need to give me a decision right now,' he said, stroking the hair back from her face. 'But please consider these options. Don't end things just because other relationships haven't worked out in the past.'

'I want this to work between us,' she said, gazing up at him.

He leaned down and kissed her gently.

'Then the details don't matter,' he said. 'Let's work our future out together.'

We do hope that you have enjoyed reading this large print book.

Did you know that all of our titles are available for purchase?

We publish a wide range of high quality large print books including:
Romances, Mysteries, Classics
General Fiction
Non Fiction and Westerns

Special interest titles available in large print are:
The Little Oxford Dictionary
Music Book, Song Book
Hymn Book, Service Book

Also available from us courtesy of Oxford University Press:
Young Readers' Dictionary
(large print edition)
Young Readers' Thesaurus
(large print edition)

For further information or a free brochure, please contact us at:
Ulverscroft Large Print Books Ltd.,
The Green, Bradgate Road, Anstey,
Leicester, LE7 7FU, England.
Tel: (00 44) **0116 236 4325**
Fax: (00 44) **0116 234 0205**

SOMETHING'S BREWING

Wendy Kremer

When Kate's job as a superstore manager comes to an abrupt end, she takes a risk and signs the lease to a seafront café. After hiring a teenage girl to work weekends, Kate is shocked to learn that her uncle is Ryan Scott, her former boss. He's tall, dark, attractive — and in Kate's opinion, arrogant. As she opens for business, she begins to see a different side to him. But with a café to run, Kate doesn't have time to think about Ryan, or any other man . . .

MEETING MOLLY

Chrissie Loveday

With £4.07 in her bank account, the rent due, and her party-planning business foundering, Sarah-Louise is forced to look for a job. Spotting one in the paper, she makes the call and soon meets Olly, who is looking after his sister's dog Molly for six months and needs someone to walk her. Sarah-Louise takes a fancy to him — but after dealing with an AWOL Molly, a jealous flatmate and a worrying attack on Olly, could the two of them possibly have a future together?

NEVER LET YOU GO

Sarah Purdue

When Sofia Garcia's fiancé Jack says he needs space and then drops off the radar, she takes up her uncle's offer of a job as a tour guide in Spain, determined to move on with her life. But when she recognises a name on her latest guest list, she can't believe it's *her* Jack, who she hasn't heard from in eight months — he's come to Spain to try to win her back. Can Sofia find a way to trust him again, and is she prepared to risk her heart once more?

THE RANSOM

Irena Nieslony

Eve Masters's life is thrown into chaos when her beloved David is kidnapped on their home island of Crete. Determined to track down those involved, Eve finds herself at odds with the police and suspecting her own friends. Then David escapes; but, ill and unable to remember who his kidnappers were, he is rushed to hospital — where someone tries to silence him for good. Can Eve get to the bottom of the mystery before the kidnappers turn their sights on her?